FAIRER THAN ANY

MAIL ORDER BRIDES OF SPRING WATER BOOK 6

KATHLEEN BALL

I dedicate this book to all the readers who encouraged me to keep going. You're the reason I keep writing.
And as always, to Bruce, Steven, Colt, Clara and Mavis because I love them.

CHAPTER ONE

*D*aisy's stomach quivered in both fear and excitement. She was in Spring Water, Texas to meet her groom. Imagine, someone wanted to marry her. She reached up and adjusted her oversized bonnet. She'd rather people stare at her for the big bonnet than for the marks on her face.

She'd answered a good deal of mail-order bride ads, but after she told them how she looked, they'd all stopped writing. But someone didn't care about that. He'd kept writing, and now she found herself on the way to her own wedding. The trip had been long, and the stagecoach was unbearably hot and dusty. Finally, they arrived at her destination and she would take her first steps in her new home. The driver turned his head from her as he held out his hand to help her down. It shouldn't have hurt — after all, she was used to such reactions — but hurt it did.

There were a few men on the boardwalk, and she wondered which one was Fletcher Taylor. Two of the men had brown hair and blue eyes. One hurried away, and the other smiled and offered his arm to the other female passenger.

Reaching deep, she found her courage and waited. The driver had put her bag down at her feet. Now she was glad it wasn't heavy. No one else waited in front of the general store. All the others on the stage had already gone. It didn't mean anything, she told herself. Fletcher was just late.

A few passersby gave her curious stares. She pretended not to notice.

"Shh," a pretty girl said. "She'll hear you."

"Hush yourself," The taller of them said. "Just look at her. I doubt anyone here is looking for a scullery maid."

The girls laughed as they went into the store. Daisy acted as though she hadn't heard them. It never helped to ask people to stop. No matter where she went, someone always had an unkind remark to make.

She peered up the street then down. Where was Fletcher? She didn't want to be still standing here when those girls came out. She bent her knees, gracefully picked up her worn bag, and strode to the end of the walk. There, in the dress store window was the most beautiful dress she'd ever seen. It was a coral pink with gorgeous lace detail. It wasn't for the likes of her, of course, but it sure was lovely. Once again, she scanned the near-empty town. All she saw were a few Union Soldiers.

There didn't seem to be a hotel in sight. Now what? If Fletcher's letters hadn't been so kind and understanding, she would have asked the other passengers where to stay before they got off. She sighed. Maybe he was on his way.

From the position of the sun, it must be well past noon. How long was she to wait? Where should she go? She peeked inside her reticule, but there was not much in it besides a few coins. Still, it might be enough for something to drink.

Picking up her bag once again, she went next door to the restaurant named The Kingsman.

She opened the door, stepped inside, and sighed in relief because it was almost empty. The table in the far corner looked good, but she needed to watch out the window for Fletcher. As soon as she was seated, a woman wearing trousers came barreling out the back.

"Howdy! I'm Shelly Kingsman." Shelly stuck out her hand, and Daisy shook it. Shelly hadn't recoiled from her. In fact, she smiled.

"I'm Daisy Weathers."

"Nice to meet ya. Would you like something to eat or drink?" Shelly's dark eyes were kind.

"Water would be wonderful. I'm waiting for someone." She tried to sound hopeful, but she was certain it didn't sound that way.

"Who are ya waiting for? I know most people here about."

"Fletcher Taylor."

"You must have missed him. He was in town about an hour ago when the stage…" Shelly narrowed her eyes. "Are you related to him?"

"No, we were to be married."

"That no-good son of a— He's a rat, all right. Let me get you some food, and then I'll take you to the Eastman Ranch where he lives."

Before Daisy had a moment to say a word, Shelly had headed into the back, probably where the kitchen was. Maybe she wouldn't bring her anything expensive. Daisy sat very still. So, Fletcher had seen her and fled. It was the worst type of blow. Her brother was right; no man would ever want her. But she thought this time it would work out. Fletcher wrote it didn't matter what she looked like.

Tears burned at the backs of her eyes, but years of practice had enabled her not to let those tears fall. She was over a week's travel from home, and she had no money.

"WHAT WAS THAT NOISE?" Georgie Eastman asked her husband.

"Probably Walter dropping something while moving into his new house," Her husband Parker said. He'd been a Captain in the Confederate Army and now was the owner of the Eastman Ranch.

"No, not that thumping sound. I thought I heard someone in distress. I'll go check." She hurried outside before Parker could stop her.

But it wasn't Walter. Georgie took one look at the scene before her and cried out in alarm. "Parker, come quick!"

When Parker exploded through the door, Georgie wasn't surprised to see the rifle in his hands.

An unkempt man had stopped the wagon in front of their house. He climbed into the back and rolled another man to the ground and then he quickly got back into the driver's seat and hightailed it out of there. He didn't even acknowledge them.

Georgie ran to the man on the ground. He was breathing, but he didn't open his eyes. He wore a filthy, tattered uniform of an ex-confederate soldier. It was so torn up she could see the bruises on his torso. There was a putrid odor, and she knew what that meant. Infection was setting in.

"Oh no, it's Jerry Sterling. I often wondered where he'd gotten to." Parker turned toward the horse corrals and yelled for the men to help him.

They hustled over and one by one, their faces became drawn as they saw their fellow soldier on the ground.

"Where should we put him?" Lex Willis asked. Lex had also served with Parker.

Parker stared at Georgie. "There's an empty house in Joy," he suggested. Joy was the freedman's area on the ranch. Parker had built the ex-slaves houses, given them jobs, and had arranged for the education of their children.

Fletcher took his hat off and slapped it against his thigh. "No good will come from putting a white man there."

Georgie shook her head. "I disagree. They wouldn't mind one bit. We all live on the ranch and pitch in where needed. Get him settled, and I'll grab Glory. She went foraging for healing plants just yesterday."

Parker nodded. "Give me a hand getting him over to Joy. Joy was a stone's throw away so they didn't have far to go.

Glory was out of her house with her herb basket before Georgie had a chance to get her. "Kent," she called.

"I know, watch the children. Can you get word to Letty we need her to look after the kids?"

"I sure will." Glory caught up with Georgie, and they both ran down the hill to Joy. There was one street in Joy, and it had ten houses on each side. Most of the people there had never lived in a real house before. They were grateful to Parker Eastman, and took pride in their homes.

Letty was already there. She knew more about healing than Georgie and Glory combined. She barely glanced up when the two women entered the house. "I sent my oldest, Hannah, to mind the children."

"Thanks, Letty," Glory said. She sniffed. "Gangrene? That smell is just awful. How bad is he?"

"I just looked him over and while most of his wounds are infected, the only gangrene is on the back of his lower leg."

Glory shook her head, making a noise of sympathy.

"Now, I have seen before where part of the leg is cut

away; taking the dead part without taking the whole leg," Letty mused. "If it doesn't work, we'll take the leg then."

"I've heard of such a treatment," Glory said. "I read about the procedure in a book." She heaved a sigh. "Madame Wigg from the Foundling Home and School is sending me replacements for all the books I lost in my travels. I can't wait to get them."

Letty nodded. "We will need laudanum; the willow bark tea won't do this time. I'll need to pack the wound with comfrey. Be sure to make an extra batch," she told Georgie. "He has numerous wounds. A body'd think the war was still going on by the looks of him."

Georgie got busy grinding and steeping the herbs. She'd make some salve and a chest plaster. He'd been coughing some, and the rattling noise he made while breathing could be lung problems.

Glory and Lettie got busy undressing and washing Jerry Sterling. Georgie had seen a lot in her life, but Jerry Sterling was by far the filthiest man she'd ever encountered. They went through buckets of water. Luckily, the children who lived in Joy were happy to help. They all especially liked Glory, their school teacher.

Sondra a woman who had lived on the ranch for a long time ran into the house. "Anything I can do?"

"Not just now." Georgie shook her head. "Go move into your new house."

"We've been living there for days now. Let me know if I'm needed." Sondra hurried back out the door, calling over her shoulder, "We have a bed." Then she was gone.

"I don't think Sondra could be subtle if she wanted to," Letty laughed.

"That's the truth," Glory agreed with a chuckle.

"Mrs. Eastman? Is one of you Mrs. Eastman?" The

wounded man tried to sit up, but Glory held his shoulders down.

Georgie stood next to him. "I'm Georgie Eastman. Parker helped to bring you here."

"Can you tell him I'm sorry? I couldn't leave my brother. I promised my ma I'd look after Bill." He coughed. "Bill was the one who dropped me off. Rolled me to the ground he did. Tell the captain I should have listened." His eyes closed, and he went limp.

"His own brother?" Georgie shook her head.

"Let's get the dead part of his leg off before he wakes up," Glory said. She opened a small bag she kept in her basket. It contained tools for surgery. She had ordered it all the way from New York City. "Ready?"

IT HAD BEEN HORRIBLE. Blood had sprayed and dripped everywhere, yet Jerry lived. And all three women were hopeful and extra glad when Iris and Mary Beth arrived to take over for a while.

Once outside, Georgie and Glory hugged Letty before she walked in the opposite direction.

As she walked home with Glory, Georgie surveyed their surroundings. The small community they'd built was everything she could have dreamed of. Parker'd had a house built for each soldier who married, and now several women and children lived on the ranch, all willing to lend one another a hand.

"I don't know about you, Glory but I'm exhausted."

"Me too. It's almost sunset. I sure hope Kent made supper."

"Your husband is a good cook, if I remember correctly."

Glory laughed. "Out of necessity, considering I couldn't

even cook when I first got here. I'll check on the patient before bedtime."

"No, you have school to teach in the morning. I can do it. I'll get you if he takes a turn for the worse."

Glory nodded. "I wonder what happened to him and to have his brother drop him here like that. There must be a long story we're bound to hear."

"He seemed anxious to get it off his mind. Of course we'll hear the whole story. Goodnight, Glory."

Georgie watched until Glory let herself into her house. It was nice to have friends.

CHAPTER TWO

*G*eorgie had just hung up her wrap when she heard another wagon coming toward the homestead. She put her wrap back around her shoulders and went back outside.

"Howdy, Georgie!" Shelly Kingsman called out as she reined in her horses.

"Hello, Shelly."

By now, many of the workers had stopped what they were doing and watched. A visit from Shelly was almost always an event.

Parker made his way to his wife's side.

"Good to see you, Shelly," he greeted.

Georgie looked at the woman sitting beside Shelly, but her bonnet mostly hid her face. She didn't raise her head at all.

"Would you like to come inside?" Parker offered.

"I have to get back, but this is Daisy. One of your men sent for her and then decided he didn't want her, or... I'm hoping he forgot she was coming today. The last part I doubt, having seen him in town earlier."

Parker gave Shelly a nod. He walked to the passenger side of the wagon, lifted Daisy down, and then lifted her bag out of the back. "We'll take good care of her."

"Daisy, it was a real privilege to spend the day with you."

"Same here, Shelly. Thank you for everything." Daisy watched Shelly drive off while shifting her weight from one leg to the other.

"Daisy, why don't we go inside? We have an extra room you can use for now," Georgie said as she held the door open for the other woman. Daisy glanced at her and smiled. Georgie hurt for the poor girl. Daisy must have had small-pox. That explained the large bonnet. Georgie wanted to go to the bunkhouse and slap Fletcher across the face.

DAISY WALKED into the nice big house trying to keep her face adverted. They would see her ugliness soon enough. The house was nice and spacious. There was cheerfulness to it. Would they send her packing when she took off her bonnet? Perhaps she should just leave it on. Back in Arkansas, she had stayed on the farm. She almost never went into town. So many had died of the disease and people hated that she survived and their loved ones were dead. Others were just cruel because of her marked face.

"Please sit down. Parker, could you pour us some coffee?" Georgie led her to pretty upholstered chair.

What was there to talk about? Her stomach churned. It was only polite to take off her bonnet, but she hadn't taken it off in public the whole trip. She sat on the edge of the seat and made sure her posture was correct. Her mother had owned two books; the Holy Bible and a book on etiquette. Both had been drilled into Daisy every day.

She put her reticule next to her on the chair. Next, she

took off her gloves and set them on top. She couldn't bring herself to take the hat off. Before the epidemic, she'd been considered to be very pretty with thick wavy blond hair. No one saw her hair anymore.

Parker came back with a tray of coffee filled cups and a bowl of sugar accompanied by a small pitcher of cream. He set the tray in front of Georgie.

"How do you take your coffee?" Georgie asked her.

"Cream please."

Georgie poured the cream in, stirred it with a spoon, and handed it to Daisy. Her hostess clearly knew etiquette too. Daisy watched as Georgie handed Parker his coffee black and then added sugar to her own.

Georgie sat back in her chair, took a sip of coffee before she spoke. "Now, tell us what happened. One of the men on the ranch sent for you?"

Daisy's face heated. "Yes, I thought I'd try to become a mail-order bride. I tried twice before, but when I described what I look like they stopped writing. I would have stopped but our farm wasn't producing as it once had, and my brother told me I was just another mouth to feed. I tried one more time, and this time the man told me the skin on my face didn't matter. We made plans, and I expected him to meet the stage coach, but he wasn't there. A man matching his description walked away, but I never thought the man I'd been corresponding with wouldn't be there so I didn't imagine that man could have been Fletcher Taylor." She took a sip of her coffee and then set the cup down.

"I waited outside the general store until some girls came by. I moved to the end of the boardwalk and waited. After a long while, I walked into the restaurant and I met Shelly. She thought maybe you could help me. I don't want to impose, but the trip cost much more than Mr. Taylor sent me. I was raised on a farm, and I know how to work. I bet there is someone looking for a farm hand in the area. I'll find employment and a place to live in a few days."

Parker stood up. "I will have a word with Fletcher."

Daisy got to her feet. "Please sir, if the man can't stand the sight of me, I'd just as well not know him." She swallowed hard. Her words had been so hard to say. She'd had such hopes this time.

"Very well, and the name is Parker, not sir. Don't you worry about staying. Georgie could use some help around here, especially since she's tending to a sick man who'd served under me."

Daisy sat back down. "That is more than kind. I tended to my mother before she died. If you need me to I could help with him."

Georgie smiled. "Let's get you settled and we can talk more in the morning."

"I am a bit weary from my day. Just show me which room and I'll be out of your way."

Georgie led Daisy to a clean and sweetly decorated room. Carrying her bag, Parker followed and then quickly left.

"I don't want you to worry," Georgie said. "We won't make you leave the ranch. Get a good night's sleep. I'll knock in a minute after I grab some warm water for you to wash up with."

Daisy turned around in a circle. The room was so big. A bright quilt covered the bed. She walked to it and ran her hand over it. Her eyes widened when she spotted the pillow. It was much grander than what she was used to but she would have liked a one-room shack with a man who loved her more.

Georgie knocked on the door and handed her a pitcher and basin.

Daisy took them and set them down. She took off her bonnet and resisted the urge to look at herself in the big mirror; she knew what she looked like. After washing and changing into her night clothes, she climbed into bed and lay down. It was a relief she wasn't looking for a safe place to hide out for the night and she'd met some very nice people. She turned onto her side.

Lord, if you have any other suggestions of how my day was good, I'd appreciate the help.

One tear fell and then another. Fletcher must have been appalled when he saw her. He must have thought... She'd thought since he'd been a soldier and had seen hurt soldiers... But it didn't matter; he saw her and didn't claim her. How could her heart feel so empty, yet so full of pain?

Lord, you know I always try to find the good so it balances the bad. There were good people in my life today but my heart aches like never before. I thought I'd grown stronger and the way people looked at me mattered less and less. I've worked through disappointment time and again with your help and I thank you for that. But this hurt feels as though it's running through my whole body, and I don't think I'll be rid of it anytime soon.

She turned onto her back and stared at the ceiling.

JERRY STERLING WOKE at the first sign of dawn just like he'd always done. It was so silent it was almost as though it was a time just carved out for him. It was special, and he coveted it. He liked to be outside, gazing at the sunrise. He always talked to the Lord at these moments.

Look after Bill for me. I'm afraid he'll end up hanging.

His leg throbbed, and it was almost unbearable, but he gritted his teeth. The front door opened and closed. It was the Negro woman, and a girl on the verge of womanhood accompanied her.

"I see you made it through the night," she said.

"Slept right through. I never got your name."

She put a bottle on the table near his bed. He'd seen it enough to know it was laudanum.

"I'm Letty. This here's my daughter, Hannah. I'll be stopping by in the morning on my way to school."

"Pleased to meet you both," he said with a nod to each.

"Hannah, you go in the kitchen and see if anything needs tending, and I'll be right along." After her daughter left, Letty poured water into a glass and helped him raise his head to drink.

"Do you teach?"

Letty smiled widely. "No, but I help Glory. She's the one who was here with the dark hair. I know how to read thanks to her." The pride in her voice was clear.

"I'm glad she's teaching free women to read. Is she teaching the men too?"

"If they want. She teaches the children during the day. She taught me when she could. Now I help her during the day and I teach the other grown people at night if they want. I'm glad most want." She put laudanum in the empty glass and filled it with water. After she stirred it, she handed it to him. She helped him keep his head up to make drinking easier.

He handed her the glass. "Thank you. I bet you're a fine teacher. Too many people nowadays trying to take advantage of anyone who can't read. The blond woman is Captain Eastman's wife?"

"Yes, that's Georgie. They don't make them sweeter. Many of us from the area have houses on the ranch. We call this area Joy. Parker keeps us safe and we have a school for the children and jobs for the men."

He could feel the drowsy effects of the medicine. "I'm glad you're safe."

"Georgie will be here in a bit to bring you some food and check your wound. I'm going to be late if I don't hurry."

"Thank you." He closed his eyes.

———

DAISY WOKE AND DRESSED. Then she put her bonnet on before she left the room. Georgie was feeding two children in the kitchen. She glanced up and smiled at Daisy.

"Good morning, Daisy. Did you sleep well?"

Daisy nodded.

"Help yourself to coffee and flapjacks. I'd do it for you, but if I take my eyes off Douglas, he'll make a run for the door. He likes to watch his pa with the horses, but he's not supposed to. He doesn't understand he could get hurt out there."

"I'm used to doing for myself." Daisy poured the coffee and put two flapjacks on her plate. She took her cup and plate and put them on the table. She was glad to see the cream, but the syrup made her smile. "I haven't seen syrup in years. What a treat."

She sat down and fixed her coffee and flapjacks to her liking. She tasted the food and closed her eyes. "Oh my, better than I remember!"

Georgie chuckled. "I felt the same way when I got here. I have a proposition for you but don't feel you must say yes. The wounded soldier is in a house in Joy, and I was wondering if you could look after him? We'd all stop in daily to help and make sure his wound is healing. It's the nights I worry about. I'm afraid he'll have nightmares and end up falling out of bed. Parker mentioned that Jerry Sterling used to cry out in his sleep often. Now before you answer let me tell you, people might talk with you being a single woman tending to a man alone and sleeping there. It's fine if you say no, really it is. Parker spent a good portion of the night there, but he didn't sleep."

"I'll do it." She almost wanted to snatch the words back, but what else could she do? She refused to go back home where people didn't celebrate the fact she survived but ridiculed her instead.

"Are you sure?" Georgie stared at her.

Daisy nodded her head. "No one knows me here so I'm not worried about the gossip. If not for my face, I'd have made a good wife. I know how to do everything on a farm, including planting crops. I'm a good cook and I'm might handy with a needle too. I can train horses and milk cows, and I have a knack with growing a garden too. It's a shame no one sees me for who I am. If I can help this Mr. Sterling, then I'd be happy to."

"You're one of the good ones, Daisy. I'm glad you're here. Sondra will be here soon. She just got married. She'll look after my boys while I settle you in."

Daisy took her last bite. "I'd best get packed back up then. Would you rather I do the dishes first?"

Georgie smiled. "Maybe I shouldn't let you go. Looks like you could be a big help here."

Daisy smiled back. She pushed away from the table and stood. It was too hard to exchange lighthearted banter. She went into the bedroom and packed. Taking a few deep breaths, she was ready. It had to be easier than being a mail-order bride. At least Mr. Sterling couldn't up and run. Cringing at her thoughts, she picked up her bag and met Georgie at the door.

Another woman stood talking to Georgie. It probably felt good to have such friends.

"Sondra, this is Daisy."

Sondra moved her head so she could look past Daisy's bonnet. "You're the one Fletcher left in town, aren't you?"

Daisy didn't know what to say. Most people looked at her in dismay, even fright but never said a word. Others called her names, but she was never expected to answer them. "I'm ready to go."

Sondra's eyes flashed in annoyance.

"I'll be back, Sondra. Thanks for looking after the boys." Georgie opened the door and indicated for Daisy to go first.

"Don't mind Sondra. She speaks before she thinks and is always putting her foot in her mouth. She mostly means well." She stopped. "All the houses in the area below are in a place called Joy. We have Freedmen and their families living in those houses. They all work and their children go to school. When I first thought of the idea, I wasn't sure it would work. People on both sides of the war had a lot of hate in their hearts. I think this has gone a long way to show we aren't so different. We all want a family, a place to feel safe, and a job. We interact more than I thought possible. I thought they might want to keep to themselves but they realized that not all white people want to keep them as slaves. We've learned to appreciate each other for our unique qualities and skills we all bring to the community." Georgie touched Daisy's arm. "The KKK isn't happy about our ranch. We have lots of guards, but I won't sugarcoat it. It could be dangerous to be here. Letty has already stopped by the house a few times so you should be fine. Letty is a bit of a leader, and if she gives her approval others follow suit."

"That's good to know. I socialize little."

"Daisy, they won't judge you. Sometimes I think they have bigger hearts than the rest. Come on it's the first house here."

Georgie didn't knock she walked right in and headed for the bedroom. Daisy followed. Mr. Sterling sat up in bed looking dazed.

"Jerry, this is Daisy. She will be a live-in help for you."

KATHLEEN BALL

Daisy didn't glance at Jerry, afraid of the disgust she'd see there.

"Daisy, nice to meet you. Thank you for offering to help. I try to be a nice man, but this pain has me as grouchy as a bear, so I apologize ahead of time."

She glanced at him, and he seemed pleasant enough. His eyes were a deep blue and his walnut brown hair needed cutting. His complexion was ruddy probably from all the time he spent in the saddle. He'd seen better days, she was sure of it. Her examination of him was stopped short when he caught her gaze and held it. He'd probably assessed her the same way. Yet he didn't look away or appear horrified.

"I'm glad you're here. I've only been here one day, but I feel the need to be doing something."

"How are you at fixing bridles? I bet I could find a few for you to work on."

He smiled. "I'd like that, Daisy."

"Parker or one of the men will be by to stock the house with food and supplies," Georgie said with a smile. "I think you two will get on just fine. If you need me I'm not far."

"Thank you for the job, Georgie," Daisy said as she walked her to the door.

"You take care, and I mean it, if you need anything at all just ask." Georgie patted Daisy's arm before she left.

Daisy stood at the closed door wondering what to do next.

STERLING WAITED for Daisy to come back in, contemplating his new nurse. What was her story? Everyone had one, and he couldn't help but wonder about hers. There was a deep sadness in her eyes, and he hurt for her. It would be nice to have company while he recovered, though. He had tried to

18

stand earlier, and it had not gone well. His recovery would take much longer than he'd have liked.

If only he could find out if his brother, Bill was all right. He could be dead or in jail by now. He and his brother were opposites. Sterling liked to weigh his options before acting, and violence was always a last resort. Bill was rash, and he didn't think twice about killing a man or harming a woman either. If only his mother hadn't asked him to keep Bill out of trouble. As far as he was concerned, he had already gone beyond what a normal person would do to look out for someone who seemed bent on ruining his life. And it wasn't like his brother had been particularly caring, though he supposed Bill could have just left him to die on the side of the road instead of bringing him to Parker's.

And their mother had made that request…

The whispered rustle of cloth caught his attention. He glanced at the door, and there stood Daisy. It was a pretty name. She seemed hesitant to enter the room and she still wore that ridiculous bonnet.

"Come on. We might as well get to know one another. I'll be out cold as soon as I have more of the medicine."

Her smile was unsure, but she walked in and sat on the wooden chair near the bed. She wasn't very tall, and she was too thin. Her blond hair hung down her back in waves but the bonnet covered the rest.

"So, you're as new on the ranch as I am. I'm glad to meet you, Daisy."

"It's nice to meet you too, Mr. Sterling."

"Call me Sterling. Your accent isn't Texan. Where in the South are you from?"

"I lived in Arkansas until recently. I lived and worked on the family farm all of my life. I'm a hard worker."

"What brings you to Texas?" She turned red and looked away. He shouldn't have pried.

"I was a mail-order bride, but he took one look and left. I told him in my letter how I looked, and he said it didn't matter…" Her voice trailed off.

"That must have been a blow. I'm sorry you were hurt. At least you're on the ranch and won't have to see the fool."

She shook her head. "He lives here. I haven't had to see him though. If it's fine with you, I'd rather not talk about it. Right now, I feel hurt and angry. But here I am, able to take care of you. I don't know too much about tinctures and such, but I tended my mother until she died." Her breath caught, and her hand flew to her mouth. Then she added hastily, "Not that you will die."

He laughed. "I sure hope not. I'd put you out of a job."

She gave him a small smile. "I think Glory will be here in a bit to check on your leg. Was it horribly hurt?"

"I was shot and then told they got the bullet out, but my leg never healed. They lied to me, Glory pulled the bullet out yesterday and had to cut away some of my leg. It had turned to gangrene. My brother drove me to Parker's house, rolled me out of the back of the wagon, and then he left. I guess we both have reason to be mad."

"Your own brother?"

He nodded. "Yes, ma'am. I'm lucky he stopped the wagon before he threw me out."

Her mouth formed an O. "You served under Parker Eastman?"

"Yes, I sure did."

"At least you know people on the ranch. That should make your stay go by faster."

He stared into her eyes. "What about you?"

"I don't know a soul, but that's fine. It seems to be that way wherever I go."

"You had smallpox."

She touched her face. "Yes I did. I was one of the few

survivors and I nursed the rest, but all people see now is how ugly my face is. Not one of them thanked me for looking after their kin. I thought I lived in a nice tightknit community until then. I had friends one day, and I became an outcast the next. It was hard to get used to."

The door opened, and Glory came in smiling. "You must be Daisy. Georgie's been singing your praises." Then she turned to him. "Hurts?"

He nodded.

"Let's take a look. Daisy, could I bother you for some hot water? If there is water in the reservoir that should do. I saw a few men loading the wagon with things to bring down this way."

"I'd be happy to."

DAISY WENT INTO THE KITCHEN, and there stood the most beautiful cook stove she'd ever seen. She'd heard about such stoves but never thought to see one in person. She put the pitcher into the water and filled it. Then she picked up the basin and some towels before she brought it all into Sterling's room. Sterling... it was an unusual name. She'd never known anyone named Sterling before.

Glory had taken off the bandage and was examining the wound. Daisy's heart dropped. It was a wound far worse than she had imagined, quite large and gaping. But it didn't look too red, so maybe that was a good thing. She heard the door open again and hurried to see who it was.

"Ma'am, I'm Ross Carter. I have supplies for you. Could I bring them in and leave them in the kitchen?" He smiled and she didn't think she'd ever seen such a handsome man before.

"That would be fine." She lowered her gaze, and adjusted her bonnet.

Ross Carter went back out the door, passing another man on the way in. "Fletcher, you can set that near the cook stove." he said to the man carrying a crate full of various things.

Daisy's eyes widened when she heard the name, and she looked up to find the man she had seen in town upon her arrival standing just inside the door.

His eyes scanned the room and lit on her. He stiffened and hastened to the kitchen area.

With a gasp of humiliation, she ran into the unused bedroom and closed the door.

She leaned her back against it trying to breathe. Was it only yesterday he'd done her wrong? A sigh slipped out. No, it was her fault. He couldn't have imagined how bad she looked. He'd probably had a good laugh with his buddies about the whole thing, though. Her hands shook, and her stomach churned. Why couldn't she get it through her head she was not wanted?

The sound of the outer door closing filtered into the bedroom, and she breathed easier. She quickly left the bedroom and went to see if Glory needed any help.

A glance at Jerry Sterling revealed him studying her with narrowed eyes.

"Are you all right? You look unsteady."

"I'm fine. I just saw the man who ran out on me is all. Somehow, I figured I wouldn't have to see him so soon. I wasn't prepared, I guess." She turned from Sterling to avoid the pity she knew she would see in his eyes. "Is there anything I can do, Glory?"

"Tomorrow I'll teach you how to clean the wound in case one of us can't get here in a timely manner. We almost all have babies, and it makes for the unexpected to happen." She smiled at Daisy. "I hope you intend to stay despite the bad experience you had."

Glory was beautiful and nice; she probably didn't know what a bad experience was. "I'm sticking around for a while at least."

"That's good to hear. Do you cook? I know Georgie sent down food, but if you don't cook—"

"I cook just fine, thank you. You've all been so nice, and I appreciate it."

A tender expression settled over Glory's features. "You're easy to be nice to. I have to see what my little ones are getting into. Letty will be back after supper to check on you two." She grabbed her bag and let herself out.

"Come, sit on the bed," Sterling said softly.

She gasped in surprise, but she did as he asked.

He drew her head down to his shoulder. "It must have been unbearable seeing the man you were to marry. I'm so sorry."

She held herself stiff at first before she relaxed, realizing he had no intention of hurting her. She couldn't remember the last time someone had tried to comfort her, and she couldn't stop the tears that sprang to her eyes. Before she knew it, she was sobbing on his shoulder. What a relief to let it out. But she only allowed the comfort to go on for a brief period before she lifted her head. "Thank you."

"We've all had some hard times," he murmured, leveling an understanding gaze on her.

She nodded and stood. Her face burned, and she couldn't look at him. "Yes, we have. What would you like for your noon meal? Are you even hungry?"

"I could eat."

"I'd best go and see what we have before asking what you'd like. I'll be back." She gave him a watery smile and hurried from the room before she burst into tears again. She leaned her back against the wall adjacent to his room. She needed to get herself together and soon. No one liked a crying woman. If only she could have stayed home. But it had been made clear to her that once her brother was married, she wouldn't be welcome at the house. She could have either fixed up a corner in the barn or gone to live in a line shack. A shiver raced along her spine.

She entered the kitchen area and halted, mouth gaping, taken aback. There wasn't an inch of counter or table space. She'd never seen so much food before. She took her time putting things away. For now, it was her kitchen and she was thrilled to set it up the way she wanted it. Her brother had insisted the farm kitchen stay the same way their mother had set it up, which had always felt a bit disorganized to Daisy.

A smile inched over her face at the discovery of two bottles of syrup. Georgie was such a kind person. Daisy craved more flapjacks, but she decided it would be too much for Sterling's stomach. Perhaps beef soup with peas and carrots for supper. She quickly made bread dough and crossed her fingers as she figured out how the stove worked for baking. It was the stove of her dreams. Others would think her silly, but the stove she'd cooked on at home would work one day and then the next her bread would be charred. Her brother had always blamed her, and she'd never even bothered to defend herself. She'd told him many times how the stove needed to be replaced or fixed. Talking to her brother was like trying to use a broken wagon; both were useless.

She then peeked in on Sterling. He seemed to be sleeping restfully. His beard was scraggly and his sun-darkened skin had a gray tint to it. He'd done some hard living, it looked like. His shoulders were wide and she bet once he had enough good food he'd be big and strong.

He was the type who had a sweetheart waiting for him.

Perhaps someone had sent a telegram for her to come. She'd want to reorder the kitchen to her own liking, and she would take over Sterling's care. Oh well, Daisy knew this wasn't permanent. But she was here now.

He moved his head, groaned, and opened his eyes. "Hello, Daisy. Watching me sleep?"

The heat flooding her face made her flustered. "I was just checking on you. How are you feeling?"

"The pain is pretty bad. It's worse than when I was shot, but it'll be worth it to keep my leg."

"I could give you laudanum."

He shook his head. "It makes me too sleepy. Maybe later. Did you find the food?"

"I did. I have some nice beef soup if you think your stomach will tolerate it."

"I'd certainly like to try. It smells good. Do I smell bread too?"

Smiling she nodded. "All stoves are different so I'm delighted it didn't end up burned. I'll be back with your soup and bread." She turned to leave.

"Daisy?"

Turning back, she waited for him to speak.

"Thank you."

A nod was the best she could manage, and then she left the room. She hadn't been thanked by a man in a long while. Happiness flowed through her. It seemed forever since she'd been happy. Actually, that wasn't true. She'd been happy when Fletcher Taylor proposed to her. She'd been excited and full of anticipation when she'd left home. As she got closer to Spring Water, though, doubts replaced the anticipation, but she still believed. She'd have made a wonderful wife. Life passed her by year after year, and soon she'd be considered a spinster. She always wanted to be a wife and mother.

Maybe God had a different plan for her.

She ladled the soup into a bowl and sliced the bread, adding that next to the bowl she'd set on the wooden tray. She added a napkin and a spoon. She'd have to find out where a cow was kept so she could make butter. Lifting the tray, she carried it into Sterling's room. He'd sat himself up, but his face appeared drawn from the exertion.

Smiling cheerfully, she set the tray on the table next to his bed. "Would you like me to help feed you?"

He scowled.

"I guess not then. Can you reach everything? I don't want to hover over you. If you need me just call." She left before he could scowl again. The Good Lord knew she'd seen enough of those lately.

CHAPTER THREE

$\mathcal{I}$t had been three days, and Sterling was tired of being in bed. He got reacquainted with his fellow soldiers and their families. It made his gut hurt. He should have had a family by now too. That had been his plan for as long as he could remember. He had a grubstake to buy land. When he was healed, he'd see what he could find.

The wives on the ranch, Mary Beth, Iris, Veronica, Glory, and Georgie were all delightful, and it pleased him at the way they included Daisy in their conversations. Kent, Willis, Max, Ross, and Parker were more than polite to her. He wasn't sure of Walter Green's new wife Sondra. She seemed to have a chip on her shoulder, and she was barely polite to Daisy. The loneliness that haunted Daisy's eyes at times was probably just a portion of what she felt.

The worst was when Joe Kelly, Noah Ward, and Fletcher Taylor came to visit. He was fine with Joe and Noah, but what had they been thinking by allowing Fletcher to tag along? Maybe he hadn't told everyone what he'd done. Sterling gave him the cold shoulder, but Fletcher didn't act as though he noticed.

The dang fool. You don't send for a woman and then reject her. Fletcher had always been immature, but this was by far the worst thing he'd ever done and what made it worse was he didn't seem to know it. He'd caused tremendous hurt and left a woman stranded with nowhere to go.

Daisy tried not to show it, but Sterling could see it upset her when Fletcher came around. Sterling sighed. He'd have to talk to Parker and ask him to keep Fletcher away. The sound of Daisy's humming as she worked in the kitchen flowed sweetly over him. She usually hummed Amazing Grace, but once in a while, she added Old Sam Tucker. She also sang a haunting ballad, the name of which he didn't know. He liked that one the best.

She had told him she'd be busy ironing and washing the kitchen floor that afternoon. Boredom plagued him until her heard her sing that song.

[1]COME OVER THE HILLS, *my bonnie Irish lass*
Come over the hills to your darling
You choose the road, love, and I'll make the vow
And I'll be your true love forever.

RED IS *the rose that in yonder garden grows*
Fair is the lily of the valley
Clear is the water that flows from the Boyne
But my love is fairer than any.

'TWAS DOWN *by Killarney's green woods that we strayed*
When the moon and the stars they were shining
The moon shone its rays on her locks of golden hair
And she swore she'd be my love forever

. . .

RED IS the rose that in yonder garden grows
Fair is the lily of the valley
Clear is the water that flows from the Boyne
But my love is fairer than any.

IT'S NOT for the parting that my sister pains
It's not for the grief of my mother
'Tis all for the loss of my bonny Irish lass
That my heart is breaking forever.

RED IS the rose that in yonder garden grows
Fair is the lily of the valley
Clear is the water that flows from the Boyne
But my love is fairer than any.

RED IS the rose that in yonder garden grows
Fair is the lily of the valley
Clear is the water that flows from the Boyne
But my love is fairer than any.

SHE SANG IT BEAUTIFULLY. Did she even know how lovely her voice was? Probably not. What had her upbringing been like? Aside from a very brief mention of having a brother and nursing her mother, she kept her past to herself. She'd never said what happened to her father or if she had any other relatives besides the brother. He sighed. She'd been able to leave her home, apparently without looking back. The past was probably best forgotten. He'd been in places where the unforgivable had happened and he hadn't been able to stop any of it. *Oh Bill, what turned you so mean?*

He swung his legs off the side of the bed. He stood every day. It hurt like the dickens, but he needed to get stronger. Hard work had built his muscles, but lack of food made him look thin. He needed to walk as soon as possible. He had enemies out there, and a man needed to have quick reflexes to stay alive.

"You're standing longer than a few days ago. I have to say I'm surprised. I've seen how much they cut into your leg. It's amazing you can stand at all. Just make sure you don't overdo it."

He sat back down, breathing hard. "I'm trying to be careful."

She laid a set of clothes on the bed. "Georgie dropped these off for you. I'll wash the ones you came in."

"You don't have to do that."

She shrugged. "I have to wash mine, anyway. Don't worry I'll check on you often."

He winced when he swung his legs up on the bed. "I know you will."

She grabbed up his dirty clothes and left the room. She was a puzzle. She probably was putting on that huge bonnet she wore. Many people were maimed in the war. A body would think people would overlook a few marks on her face, but it didn't sound as if people were kind to her.

He shook his head. Every person still alive after the War Between the States was blessed. Too many had died. Life had certainly changed. He'd been a rascal, in his brief youth before the war and had still been finding his way when it started. He and his brother Bill signed on as soon as they could. They'd been looking forward to the great adventure.

Their time in the war had been anything but. That was a heavy cross to bear. Man was not brought into the world to kill. Brother against brother was what people often said about the war. Whole families were destroyed as they took sides against each other.

Fletcher should be horse whipped for what he had done to Daisy. She tried to smile and be cheerful, but he'd heard her crying in her bed last night. If Fletcher had changed his mind, he should have had the courage to face her and tell her and make sure she had a place to stay.

He shook his head. Daisy was as sweet as the day was long. He had the feeling her brother was no prize either. Else, why would he have allowed her to leave? She'd jumped a few times when asked to do something by a man. They didn't notice, but he had. Too bad he had to go back after Bill as soon as he could sit a horse. His body felt much older than his years and settling down appealed to him.

Lord, look after that brother of mine. He doesn't use the good sense you gave him. Being an outlaw will bring him nothing but trouble. It was right cruel of him to dump me from the wagon and go but at least he brought me to a place where I could get help. I'm hoping and praying he'll change his ways. And Lord, if you could bring Daisy some happiness, that would be real nice.

WASHING CLOTHES WAS HOT, sweaty work. The sun in Texas seemed to beat down on her much hotter than in Arkansas. She hung the sheets first and almost screamed when she turned around and there stood Fletcher. She jumped and took a step back.

"I thought you'd go back home." He stared at her, his gaze hard as flint.

"No, I don't have but a bit of money. Not enough to even buy a meal." Her eyes narrowed before she glanced away from him. The way he looked at her made feel dirty.

"I could come up with the money, but you'd have to earn it."

"You need your clothes washed?"

He was silent until she looked at him.

"I was thinking the only thing women like you are good for is being friendly to a man in the dark. It's where you'll end up anyway."

Her face heated as her heart pounded painfully against her chest. How could he stand there after saying such a thing? "I'd appreciate it if you'd leave me alone."

"I paid good money to bring you out here. You owe me, and if you can't pay me back one way, you'll have to do it another more personal way. Think about it. I'll be back tonight." He sneered before he turned and walked away.

She wanted to drop to the ground and sob. With arms that felt like wood, she grabbed an article of clothing and hung it up. She kept going until she was done. She tried to put all thoughts out of her head, but she couldn't ignore Fletcher.

She hadn't seen any firearms in the house, but she'd look. She wouldn't say anything, though. This was her problem, and she wasn't about to ask for help. He probably wouldn't even show up. Her bottom lip quivered. No... He'd be there. He wasn't the first man to make such a suggestion, but she always had her home to go back to. She had no home here. As bad as her brother could be, he wouldn't have allowed her to come to harm.

Maybe she should go to town and send him a telegram. He could afford the price of a ticket for her to come back. She drew a shaky breath. Except...she didn't have the money to send a telegram, and he was probably glad she was gone.

Dropping down onto the back doorstep, she put her head in her hands. She'd been trying to help those around her when she contracted smallpox. No one wanted to care for her. It had always been that way. She gave so much more than she ever got back. Her brother said she was a sucker being so giving to others. She'd given so much she almost died and was never thanked for her sacrifice. Why did some think they were entitled to take and take? She sighed. It was her own fault; she couldn't stand to see others suffer when she could ease their suffering.

She'd swear she wouldn't do it again but she couldn't help it. There were too many in need. But no one remembered her good deeds when she was in need of help. The hurt went soul deep, and she felt worthless and used. One should give freely without expectation of reward but no matter how many times she told herself those words she couldn't get rid of the hurt.

She stood and went into the house. Sterling would be hungry.

SOMETHING WAS WRONG. Daisy hardly acknowledged a word he said. She didn't have her usual smile for him either. Was she tired of taking care of him? He wouldn't blame her; he was practically helpless.

Her eyes were troubled when she came in to take away the tray.

"Daisy?" He asked, leaning forward to see her better. "Is everything—"

"Don't," she answered sharply but with emotion in her voice. "Everything is fine."

Clearly, something was wrong, though. "Daisy…"

"No," she insisted. "I promised myself I wouldn't cry, and I would stand strong. It's my problem and I have to take care of it. Did you have a gun when they brought you here?"

Her words were said in earnest, and that chilled him. What was going on? "Daisy, why would you need a gun?"

"No reason, I just like to know that I can protect myself it came to it. It doesn't matter, I suppose. Glory will be here soon. School should let out. She'll be happy to see your wound healing. I need to wash up the dishes. I'll be back."

Something had happened, and he did not understand when, where, or what. But what could it be? A gun was serious. He mulled it over but never came to any conclusion.

Then she was back. "I brought you some water." She placed the glass on the bedside table. She turned to leave, but he reached out and took her wrist, stopping her.

She'd never be able to play poker; she wore her feelings and she was easy to read. "Daisy, tell me what's wrong."

She pulled her wrist from him. "I'm just trying to come to terms with the way my life is changing. The path I will take wouldn't be the path God put me on, but I have little choice. I suppose we all end up doing things to survive. You needn't worry about me. I'll be right here taking care of you until you're able to be on your own." Her smile flickered and dimmed.

"I'm here if you want to talk." The gentleness in his voice surprised him. There hadn't been room for gentle in his life in a long time.

"I thank you for your concern." Her eyes watered before she turned and hurried from the room.

Something was going on, and it was happening here on the ranch. Daisy had hardly left the house let alone the ranch. If he wasn't stuck in this bed, he'd be able to find out. The front door opened, and he heard Glory greet Daisy.

Glory entered the bedroom with a basket of herbs. Her knowledge impressed him. Kent Sandler was a lucky man.

"How are you today, Sterling?" She smiled and put her basket on the chair next to the bed.

"Fair to middling. How long before I can walk?"

She smiled. "You're an eager, one aren't you? I don't blame you, but it'll be a few months. I just heard you've been standing. You're making progress faster than I had hoped."

"Will I be able to sit a horse again?"

"It might be hard to get on and off but I don't see why not, eventually. It takes time to heal."

Eventually… that seemed like a long time. Suddenly he didn't want to talk about his injury. "How's that husband of yours? He treating you right?" he teased.

"He is the sweetest man I know." Her face glowed.

She removed his bandage and nodded as if pleased. "No infection. I think we don't have to worry so much about that from now on." She reached into her basket and drew out a jar of green ointment.

"That makes a lot of the pain go away."

"That's good since you didn't want laudanum after the first few days."

He sighed. "I've seen too many addicted to it. That and morphine. Men will kill to get their hands on it. I never want to need something that badly."

"I don't blame you." She slathered the comfrey mixture on him and then put a fresh bandage on it. "Does the willow bark tea help at all?"

"It takes the edge off. I'll survive." He smiled.

She returned his smile. "I know you will." She lowered her voice. "Why does Daisy look as though she's ready to cry?"

"I wish I knew," he whispered back.

"Well, we'll do what we can to cheer her up. The humiliation of your groom not claiming you must be an awful thing."

"It couldn't have been good."

"I have to get back to the children." She reached out and

gave his hand a squeeze before she picked up her basket. "Have a nice evening."

"You too, Glory."

He watched her leave. It must be wonderful to be blessed the way she and her husband were. He'd missed out on that. He'd never have a family of his own. Wanted men didn't have the luxury of settling down. Friendships made were fleeting, and there could never be a sweetheart. It was a life he hated and if not for Bill, he'd have nothing to do with it.

Bill must have known where Parker was for some time, and yet he'd never said a word. He was selfish, very selfish. He didn't care; he took and took until there wasn't anything left. Then he'd move on looking for something he could steal.

Sterling had tried everything to get Bill to give up his life of crime. But there was no helping a person who didn't want to be helped.

What about Daisy, though? He couldn't help her either, could he? What did she need a gun for? If he never held one again, he'd be grateful. Unfortunately, that would never happen. He wanted to explain things to Parker. They'd been close during the war, and Parker had been vocal about his disapproval of Bill.

Sterling wished he'd had the choice to listen to Parker, but that hadn't been possible.

DAISY HELD A COOL, wet cloth against her eyes. Even Glory felt sorry for her and was talking about her. Staying at the ranch in the long run probably wouldn't work out. She'd run into people who talked about her every day. At least on the farm she had months where she saw no one but her brother, his fiancée, and a couple hands. They never even gave her a second look.

How could she have been so stupid to believe that someone wanted her? It was the wanting something so bad that kept her from realizing it couldn't be true. At least she was kept busy helping Sterling, and it kept a roof over her head and food in her stomach. Working for room and board wasn't horrible. Maybe she could take in some wash to earn a little money.

Upon putting the cloth down, she realized her hands were shaking. Supper had been served and eaten, and the kitchen was spotless. Checking on Sterling would have to wait until her eyes weren't so red. He already felt sorry for her, and she couldn't bear pity.

Would Fletcher knock on the door? Tonight was the first time she'd locked the doors. She usually didn't even bolt the shutters closed but tonight she did that also. The shadows cast from the hurricane lamp had her thinking of the things Fletcher could possibly want. Not knowing about such things made everything worse. Her imagination was too vivid for her own good.

Hopefully Sterling was asleep. But if not, perhaps it was dark enough and he wouldn't see how puffy her eyes were. She stood and tiptoed to his room. He looked much younger when he slept. He must carry too many burdens.

Lord, please help Sterling heal in mind, spirit, and body. There are times he seems troubled, and maybe you could take some of the trouble away. Please watch over me tonight. I'm scared, and I don't know what to do. I don't want to just go along with Fletcher's plan. But I don't want to scream and disturb everyone.

She jumped when she heard a knock at the door. Her heart beat so fast she thought it just might give out. Resigned, she went to the door and opened it. Letty's husband Darrius was there holding a rifle. Opening the door wider, she let him in.

"I'll be staying here tonight."

Her eyes widened but words failed her.

"Are the shutter's closed?"

She nodded. "How?"

"Letty heard what Fletcher said. We waited for one of the men to come and guard you or for Fletcher to get kicked off the ranch. We finally figured you didn't tell anyone. I'm here to help."

Daisy's shoulders relaxed, and the pain in her neck lessened. "I don't know what to say."

"Say goodnight. I'll bed down here in front of the stove. Don't worry, I'm a light sleeper."

"You're going to make me cry again."

Darrius' brow furrowed. "Why do I make you cry?"

"No one has ever tried to protect me before. Thank you." She went into her room before she made more of a fool of herself. She left her clothes on and got under the covers. Any little noise, and she cringed. Finally, the knock she waited for came. She went to the door to her room and inched it open.

Fletcher sounded mad and he cursed at Darrius. He even threatened to kill Darrius.

Darrius closed the door in Fletcher's face and locked it. He stood in front of it with his rifle ready for almost an hour.

Daisy thought to stand with him, but she didn't know what to say to him. He'd probably feel he'd have to say words of comfort or something. It would be too awkward. It wasn't until she saw Darrius go back to his pallet that she curled herself into a ball on the bed. What would happen tomorrow?

---

1. Red is the Rose An Irish folk song Writer and composer unknown

CHAPTER FOUR

*L*etty bustled into Sterling's room with a cup of coffee in her hand. "Good morning! How's the patient today?" She set the coffee on the table. "You have a choice of eggs and ham or flapjacks."

Where was Daisy? He stopped himself from asking. It wasn't his business.

"Eggs would be great. Thank you, Letty."

She smiled. "I'll get to making them right away." She left as fast as she'd come in.

He heard voices and one was a man's. What was going on? Where was Daisy? A frown settled on his brow. Maybe he'd gotten too used to having Daisy around.

A tall, muscular man with dark skin entered the room. He walked to the bed and held out his hand. "I'm Darrius, Letty's husband. It's nice to meet you, Sterling."

Sterling admired the show of confidence. He accepted the man's hand, and they shared a handshake. "It's good to know you. I'm a big admirer of your wife. You're a lucky man."

"Truer words were never said. I just wanted to meet you, seeing as you're a neighbor."

"Stop by anytime."

Darrius gave him a quick nod before he left. Sterling heard Letty and Darrius talking in low voices, and then her husband left.

He reached over and picked up his coffee. He took a sip and smiled. Her coffee was almost as good as Daisy's. His scowl returned. Why couldn't he get Daisy off his mind?

An hour later, Daisy still hadn't come to his room. Irritated and worried, he stood and clenched his jaw because of the pain. Being helpless wasn't something he was used to. She was in the house, he heard her cleaning. He'd have to call to her. Normally he tried not to be a bother, but something wasn't right.

"Daisy!" His voice sounded gruff with his pain.

She appeared at his door and without saying a word, she helped him onto the chamber pot. She barely glanced at him, which was just as well. She stepped out of the room to give him privacy.

When he called her again, he was standing next to the bed.

"I'll empty it."

"Daisy, wait. Could you help me back into bed? I think I over did it. I don't want to chance a fall."

It was obvious that she had something on her mind. She hardly interacted with him.

"Thank you. Daisy, can I ask you something?"

Her lips pursed. "What?"

"What is going on? I know there's some trouble, but I don't know what. Are you all right?" He tried to make his voice as gentle as he could.

"Let me empty the pot, and I'll come back in and we can talk." She gave him the quickest smile he ever saw and then frowned as she left.

He heard the back door open and close and then he heard the front door open and close. What was going on?

Parker walked into his room and sat down on the chair. "We have a problem buddy. Your brother and Fletcher are now riding together. I heard about the threats he made, and I was on my way to tell him to get off the property but Noah told me. I guess Bill stayed around the area. He probably wanted to be sure you would make it."

Sterling's jaw dropped momentarily. "What? What threats?"

Daisy stood in the doorway turning paler by the minute. "I didn't want to worry you. It's my problem."

Parker stood up. "Daisy, take a seat. First, we consider everyone on the ranch to be family. If one of us has a problem, we all have a problem. We stay safe that way. I'm glad Darrius stayed here last night. Fletcher had no right to make any threats to you, and if anything like that happens again, I want to know about it."

Daisy flinched but then nodded.

"Will someone tell me what happened?" Sterling was getting mad.

Daisy took a deep breath. "I was hanging the sheets yesterday, and Fletcher came up behind me. He startled me. He said he thought I would have gone home by now, and I told him I didn't have the money to go back home." She swallowed hard, and her face went from being pale to being scarlet. "He told me he'd give me the money, but I had to earn it. Stupid me, I offered to do his wash, but that wasn't what he had in mind. I told him no, and he insisted I pay him back for the money he sent for me to come out. He told me he would come and get me when it was dark to do what he planned. I didn't know what to do."

"It's a good thing Fletcher left," Sterling declared. She jumped; he must have looked as livid as he felt

She nodded. "Letty heard Fletcher threaten me, and she had her husband stay here. Fletcher knocked on the door, and Darrius sent him away." She put her face in her hands. After a moment, she sat up straight. "I'm glad to hear he's gone."

"That's why you asked about my gun."

"I'll make sure she has one by this afternoon," Parker said. "Fletcher was always a loose cannon. He tried to corner Sondra and then claimed she was wrong about his intentions. I should have listened."

"Riding with Bill will bring him nothing but trouble. I know." He pounded a fist against the mattress. "I feel so useless in this bed."

"Do you still have your guns?" Parker asked.

"Yes, why?"

"You can protect Daisy. I'll make sure everyone knows to sound the alarm if they see Fletcher. Sterling, you can guard her at night. The houses are extra sturdy. I didn't want the KKK to get into any of them."

"Where are your guns?" Parker asked.

"In the drawer."

Parker walked to the table and pulled open the drawer. He lifted out the pair of six-shooters still in the holster. "I'll make sure you have enough bullets. I'm sorry about what Fletcher did, Daisy. If you need anything, everyone on the ranch will help."

"Thank you, Parker." Her voice wobbled.

He touched her on the arm before he left. She appeared calmer.

"I wish you had told me, but I understand why you didn't. Bill and Fletcher never got along. Bill was wounded early on and was out of the fighting for a long time before he returned. I thought maybe he deserted. My mother spoiled Bill and never held him accountable for his actions. Those two are not a good combination, but Bill will have to stand on his own feet. I won't be able to pull him out of trouble. I never went on raids with him and his gang, but I never stopped them either. I was there to keep Bill from getting hanged. It burdened my conscience something awful. I heard rumors of what they did, but I also knew they wouldn't hesitate to turn on me and kill me."

"Your heart must have been very heavy the last few years." Her eyes glistened with tears.

"Ever since we signed up for the war, it's been tearing me apart. I promised my ma, I'd watch out for Bill. She cried hard when she asked and made me swear I would. I've tried my best to keep my promise." He sighed. His heart *was* heavy, and his soul was shredded. A wave of shame swept over him. He should have done more to stop Bill. Now that Fletcher was with Bill, there would be no way to keep him from the evil ways he desired.

As if she knew his inner turmoil, one of her tears rolled slowly down her cheek.

"I'm as responsible for all the damage they have done. I could have gone to any sheriff, but I didn't. I kept my mouth shut. I begged God to help me, but the raiding went on and on."

"You're here now," she said softly. "Perhaps God answered your plea. Hopefully you'll be able to put some shreds from your soul back together. We've all been in positions we wish we weren't. Your mother couldn't have known what her request would lead too. You're a good man, Sterling." She stood and gave him a long look. "You've fulfilled your promise. You can't risk yourself to help someone who doesn't want to be helped."

"I know, everything you've said is true and my mind accepts it but my heart remembers my mother's plea as if it was just yesterday. I can still hear her voice and it takes over. Before I know it I'm riding with them."

"I hope you'll be able to rest your struggles a bit while you're here." She gave him a smile filled with compassion before she left the room.

He couldn't help but worry about Bill. Some men he'd ridden with were as mean as Satan but Fletcher could be worse. Bill always liked to be in charge, and Fletcher didn't enjoy taking orders. It also didn't sit well that Fletcher had threatened Daisy. They'd have to come up with a plan so she was never alone.

DAISY SAT at the table peeling potatoes and pondering her earlier conversation with Sterling. He had so many burdens to bear, though his were mostly on the inside as opposed to her burden, which was apparent to all. But he'd never avoided looking at her as her brother had often done. It had come to the point where his future wife refused to eat if Daisy was sitting at the table.

It hurt, but having her brother agree hurt even more. If not for her faith, she would have thrown herself off a cliff a long time ago. Being here was so different. Everyone seemed to appreciate her help. It was such an uplifting experience. There were good people here. They didn't judge people by looking at them, they looked deeper to find the good in a person. How different the world would be if everyone did it that way.

She tried not to judge people, but sometimes it was hard to get past how a person dressed or whether that person had bathed in the last month. She couldn't avoid seeing what was in front of her. There were so many different people in the world. If she just went by looks alone, she'd never get to know anyone.

If someone was dressed in expensive clothing, she thought herself not as good as them. If a person was dressed in rags, her brother would have called them lazy, not working hard enough to have some coin in their pockets. There were so many unique reasons why someone was poor, a widow with kids and no income, inability to find work, crop failures, sickness. She knew because she had taken the time to know and to help. Poor people were not lazy and they did not drink their pay away.

She should give rich people a chance, she surmised. They might be nice but she'd never know unless she got to know one—or at least tried. Not that they'd talk to her now. They usually steered clear of her. Look at Letty and her family; they were educated. People would assume because of the color of their skin they couldn't read. She'd heard people claim the freedmen to be like children that needed the shelter of a plantation.

She'd never met an Indian, but she'd seen how they were treated. Did Northerners think Southerners evil? Men highly prized a beautiful woman with little to no opinions. Did men think of women as children too? It seemed like it at times.

The man, who had a good job, was considered better than another man who was also doing honest work but perhaps in a more menial position. If Sterling ended up with a limp, would people think less of him? That he was a man to be pitied? Love thy neighbor as thyself. There wasn't much of that going on in the world, except here on the Eastman Ranch. People had been kind to her. Did the freedmen on the ranch think themselves better than the freedmen in a place near town, a shanty town called Liberty?

She tried never to feel better than, but she often felt less than others. Imagine everyone being kind to one another.

Being here on the ranch filled her with hope, and somehow she felt as though her faith had been renewed. She wanted to meet the reverend but she wouldn't be able to attend services until Sterling was healed.

After she put the potatoes on the stove to boil, she peeked in on Sterling. He was napping. She'd keep him in her prayers. There was a knock on the door, and fear filled her as she went to answer it. Cautiously, she opened the door, but when she saw the women, she opened it wide and invited them all to come inside.

Glory, Georgie, Violet, Iris, Mary Beth, and Letty all filed in, and as Daisy started to close the door, Sondra pushed her way in. Looking around in dismay, she realized she didn't have enough chairs for the group.

Georgie took her hand. "We're all here for you. When Parker told me what happened with Fletcher, I wanted to take a broom to that man. I would have too, but he'd already left."

"Are you all right?" Mary Beth asked.

"Nervous, but fine. Letty's kind husband stayed here last night and guarded me." Daisy smiled at Letty. "I'd offer you all coffee, but we don't have enough cups."

Violet laughed. "It's a common occurrence. We didn't come for refreshments. We just want you to know you can count on us."

"If you need anything at all don't hesitate to ask," Iris added.

Glory rolled up her sleeves. "While I'm here, I'll check Sterling's leg."

"He was sleeping a minute ago," Daisy said.

"It's fine. He can go back to sleep when I leave." Glory, with her basket on her arm, disappeared into the bedroom.

"So, Daisy," Sondra drawled. "Any plans to marry or are you just going to live in sin?"

Iris gasped. "She is not living in sin. She is taking care of an injured man. Where did you hear otherwise, or did you make it up?"

Sondra shrugged. "A woman who lives with a man alone is no better than a—"

"Sondra, that's enough," Georgie reprimanded.

Daisy schooled her expression as she'd done so many times before. She found out early on that if she cried or looked upset, the bullying would keep going on. She racked her brain for something to say to change the conversation but the only word that echoed in her head was the one Sondra got cut off from saying: whore.

"You's a fool, Sondra, and a troublemaker too," Letty scolded. "Things haven't been easy for Daisy, yet she still is a sweet woman with a big heart."

Sondra glared at Letty and then smiled maliciously. "Maybe she's sweet on the inside but from where I'm standing, she—"

Georgie grabbed Sondra's arm and yanked her out of the house. The rest of the women looked decidedly uncomfortable as they followed.

Daisy swallowed hard. So much for her hopeful feeling. She put a pot on to boil some water so she could make herself a cup of tea. It would give her something to do while Glory was still in the house. Daisy needed to stay busy, tears threatened from being ambushed. Sondra was probably right; people must think her a loose woman. But there would also be those who would think Sterling would be too repulsed to touch her.

"His leg looks good. I have to run," Glory said. "Are you truly all right?"

"I am. I didn't get much sleep last night."

Glory smiled. "It's not a wonder. Take care."

Daisy was silent as she watched her leave. As soon as the

front door closed, Daisy locked it and dashed into her room. Tears fell. She tilted her head back trying to stop them from flowing but it was no use.

Why? What had she ever done to Sondra? She'd only met her once. Sondra and Georgie were good friends. Had they been talking about her? What she wouldn't give to be pretty. Too many took their looks for granted. She just wanted to be normal.

After taking a few deep breaths, she got herself together and went to the kitchen. She had supper to finish. Shepard's pie was one of her favorites. After she got it all prepared, she put it in the oven and then poured the water for her tea.

It had thrilled her when she saw it in the pantry. She hadn't had tea in a few years. She closed her eyes and enjoyed each hot sip. She couldn't rely on the people of the ranch to come to her aid. All her thoughts about not judging people were simplistic and juvenile. She knew better than most how it would never work or come to be. Her mother used to say if you can't say something nice, then don't say anything. Good advice.

She dabbed her eyes with a wet cloth as the pie baked. Her inner turmoil was still there, but she managed to look serene, at least she hoped she did.

THE FOOD WAS DELICIOUS, and he savored every bite. Daisy was a good cook. He sat back against his pillow and frowned. Something wasn't quite right with her. He didn't know what it was, unless it had something to do with the women all leaving in a hurry. It was impossible to imagine Daisy insulting them.

He watched as she came through the doorway and lifted his tray off his lap. She didn't make eye contact with him at all. What could have happened now? He knew he hadn't said anything wrong. Maybe she was tired of taking care of him.

"Daisy?"

"Hmm?" She didn't stop to see what he wanted.

"Never mind."

She didn't nod or indicate that she even heard him. He needed out of this bed. There weren't any windows in the bedroom and he missed the outdoors. He reached over and picked up his leather holster. Most men didn't have two guns but he could shoot with either hand, and it had gotten him out of a few situations. He wasn't so sure it wasn't one of the men in Bill's gang that shot him in the leg. They were galloping behind him as the sheriff chased them.

The poor sheriff had been shot out of his saddle. Sterling closed his eyes and tried to blot out the memory. *Maybe he didn't die. Maybe someone found him in time.* It was in the moment when he saw the sheriff hit dirt that he decided enough was enough. He couldn't live his life according to a promise he had made to his mother. He was going to cut loose. No sooner had he had the thought when then there was a searing pain in his lower leg.

When they stopped, Bill looked at the wound, wet it with a bit of water, and tore one of Sterling's shirts into bandages. "Looks like it's hardly nothin'. I'll get the bullet out when we stop for the night." Bill swung back up into his saddle and took off, leaving him there.

It took a bit of doing, but Sterling managed to get on his horse and follow the men. He was just grateful a posse wasn't after them. If one had been, he'd have been caught for sure.

He had known where they were headed and estimated he was a good hour behind them. When he rode into their hideout in the hills, he saw a few of the men exchanging unhappy looks. Bill didn't even get up from the ground to help Sterling down off the horse. He was disgusted with himself for being blind to the way Bill treated him.

Later that night, Bill dug into Sterling's flesh with a knife, guided only by the flames of the fire. He said he got the bullet, and he wrapped Sterling's leg back up. A few days went by, and as Sterling weakened, he realized Bill hated him. Why hadn't he seen that look in his brother's eyes before?

Why Bill brought him to the ranch, he did not understand. Maybe his conscience got to him. Perhaps it was one of the gang members. Either way, he was through with looking out for his brother. He'd talk to Parker after he was all healed up and see about a job.

He stared at his guns. He wouldn't mind hanging them up for good.

Someone knocked on the front door, and he felt useless once again. Daisy shouldn't have to face danger. He relaxed when he heard Parker's voice.

Finally, the tall man walked into the bedroom. "Got those bullets I promised you." Then he lowered his voice. "Noah heard a rumor in town today that there would be some trouble on the ranch tonight. I'll need you and Daisy to stay in your rooms and away from any windows. No lamps either. Show Daisy how to use the gun if you have to. I need to hurry back and secure my family. Keep the both of you safe."

Parker didn't wait for a reply. He was gone before Sterling thanked him.

Daisy came in and handed him a cup of coffee. She eyed his guns and then stared at him.

"Parker thinks there might be some trouble tonight. If you need to do anything, do it before dark. No lamps, and we need to stay in our rooms."

Her eyes widened. "You're not kidding, are you?"

"No, honey, I'm not."

"It'll be dark soon," she fretted. "I have the kitchen cleaned. I'll just pour myself some coffee and then head into my bedroom. I'll double check the doors and windows. I'm so sorry. This is all my fault. We all know what my future will eventually be and I was too proud to allow Fletcher to touch me." She dashed out of the room before he could tell her how wrong she was.

Is that what she really thought? He'd make sure such a future wouldn't be hers. She was too sweet to live her life that way. Fletcher and Bill really needed to be caught.

CHAPTER FIVE

*D*aisy shook uncontrollably. The shocking noise of a rifle cracking as it was fired scared her. It sounded close too. Why did Fletcher want to hurt her so badly? What had she done to attract his wrath? Now she'd put others in danger too. All she wanted was someone to love her but now she knew for sure it was an impossible dream.

Another shot split the silence, and it sounded close. She jumped up, grabbed the quilt off her bed and ran into the other bedroom. It was dark, but her eyes had grown accustomed to the lack of light. Sterling was sitting up with both guns and the bullets on his lap. His chest was bare and she tried not to look. She didn't want to cross any lines.

"Come get into bed with me."

She didn't even think about how it would look, she eased onto the side next to the wall, trying not to disturb his leg. Somehow, she found herself under his quilt too. She put her bed covers on top and brought it up to her chin to cover herself.

"Did, did you hear the shots? They sounded so close." She held in a whimper.

"I heard them, but they aren't near Joy yet. We should be fine. I've got my guns."

His nickel plated pistols gleamed as though he'd rubbed them until they gleamed.

"I'm thinking my welcome has run out. I couldn't bear it if someone got killed because of me."

His head turned until he was looking into her eyes. "This is in no way your fault. Fletcher had a responsibility to you as his mail-order bride. Listen if he changed his mind, he still should have made sure you had enough money to get back home. He never was the responsible type of man. He enjoyed killing the men of the northern army. The rest of us did it because we were commanded to. Not one of us had the stomach for it, but we did our duty.

"You can't blame him for not wanting me. I was up front with him about my scars from smallpox. I thought I would finally have a home, a husband and children." She shrugged her shoulders. "But it's not to be, I suppose. Now I must find work once you're able to get around."

There was pounding on the front door, and she tensed. "Do you think I should see who it is?"

"No. If it was someone we knew they'd have shouted out to us."

He turned and stared at the doorway.

She liked his strong, squared chin. His shoulders looked more muscular than before. At least he was putting some weight one. Had he broken his nose at some point? Was that why it seemed a bit crooked?

A sigh slipped out. The right thing to do was to walk out of the house and leave with Fletcher. But she was a coward. She couldn't bring herself to do it.

The knocking stopped, and Sterling reached behind

her and guided her head to his shoulder. She moved closer to him. His body was warm, and he gave her a sense of security. She shouldn't be in his bed. It was improper, and people were already talking about them. How did one find joy and hold on to it? Closing her eyes, she listened to his heartbeat and the way he breathed. He smelled like soap.

It would be so easy to pretend he was hers, but he wasn't and she couldn't lie next to him. Getting fanciful never helped it only hurt.

A loud bang sounded against the house right near her. She jumped and let out a cry. Sterling held her closer.

"Who is out there and how are they getting so close to this house? I thought we were being guarded. I wish I were a man and could run out there with guns blazing."

"Gun's blazing?" He chuckled. "We're better off here for now. I wish I was healed and whole so I could go and get rid of whoever is out there."

"I brought all this danger to the ranch. They'll be happy when I'm gone." She bit her lip. The thought of leaving left her feeling empty. She didn't have a place in the world.

Lord, please keep us safe tonight. I shouldn't have ever left the farm. But I didn't want to move out of my home and into a line shack. How could my brother have gone along with his fiancée's ideas? Didn't he know how tiny and cold the line shack was? I already know the answer. He can't stand to look at me either. I haven't seen one perfect person. There always seems to be a flaw but only my flaws matter. I'm surprised Sterling can look at me day after day. I know I'm feeling sorry for myself again. Please help us stay safe tonight.

Daisy pulled away from Sterling and put as much room between them as she could. "If I learn how to handle your guns tomorrow night, I might sleep in my room. I don't enjoy being a bother."

"You could never be a bother." A slight smile touched his lips. "Have you ever been kissed?"

"Of course not." She turned her back to him and lay silently as tears came. Why had he asked? He knew that people went out of their way to avoid her. Oh. she'd been kissed plenty in her dreams. But it was time to grow up and put her dreams away. She couldn't change how she looked, so she might as well make the best life she could for herself.

The heat from his body cloaked her. He ran his hand up and down her arm and it felt nice, too nice. Part of her wanted to scream for him to stop, and the other part wanted to savor the experience and remember it, to know what it felt like to be so close to a man. Yes, she had to stop her yearnings, but she wasn't sure how.

If one more person told her that life wasn't fair, she'd scream. She'd heard it from too many people, and it was easy for them to say. It was their way of saying she needed to accept her lot in life. She thought she had when she lived on the farm. She didn't have to go to town except to attend church services, and she usually made certain she was the last one in and the first out. She watched families and couples interact. She also watched a few men who had wanted to court her. They had stopped even saying hello.

Children would turn around trying to get a good look at her. She wanted to get a hat with a veil to wear but it hadn't been in her budget.

"Daisy?" His soft voice startled her, bringing her out of her thoughts.

"Yes?"

"I didn't mean to upset you. Go on and get some sleep. I'll stay up and keep watch."

She started to get up, but his hand stilled her.

"Stay here and sleep. I want you where I can see you."

Slowly she nodded and lay back down. He inched over

until he was next to her again. He rubbed her back and she drifted to sleep.

DAISY'S EYES OPENED, and she jumped. Sondra stood leaning against the bedroom doorway as though she'd been there for some time. She taunted Daisy with a knowing smile.

Daisy's first thought was to get out of bed but there was a weight trapping her legs. She closed her eyes. This could not be happening. Why couldn't it be Letty who came in first?

"Sterling, wake up."

He groaned and put his arm around her waist, trapping her further. Gritting her teeth, she started to push him off her.

"Just one more minute, don't leave me," he mumbled.

Daisy glanced at Sondra, who just grinned at them with her arms folded in front of her.

"Sterling, you're too heavy on me. Please wake up."

"Umm, last night," he said in suggestive, pleasured voice. He jerked away and stared at Daisy. "I thought you were someone else."

Her face burned more than ever. "Of course. We have company." She tried to sound as though everything was fine, but his words echoed in her heart. *I thought you were someone else*. He had a lover somewhere.

Daisy pulled away and landed in the tiny space between the bed and the wall. She was hopeless, and Sondra kept staring. Daisy grabbed the quilt and twisted and turned until she was standing next to the bed.

"If you take anymore covers Sondra will see something I'd rather she didn't."

Daisy gasped and threw the quilt at him before she rounded the bed and ran out the door. If only she'd had the courage to knock Sondra down. Daisy hurried into her room and closed the door behind her. There wouldn't be enough time for her to gather her thoughts. She washed her face, using the water from the night before and got dressed. Her faded calico would look even worse next to what Sondra was wearing. Why was she so dressed up?

Irritable, she opened the door and rushed into the kitchen. She put the coffee on and made herself breathe slower. Then she got warm water from the reserve and carried the pitcher toward Sterling's room.

"Sondra you're still here? Did something happen last night? I heard shots." Daisy pushed past her and put the pitcher and basin on the table next to Sterling.

"A couple new men Parker hired, got drunk and started shooting at the stars. I came to check on you, but you didn't answer the door."

Daisy's jaw dropped. "Why didn't you identify yourself? You scared me witless."

"Obviously." Sondra stared at Sterling and then switched her gaze to Daisy. "I know you haven't been here very long but we are fine, respectable people trying to make a life and raise families. Your behavior won't be tolerated."

Sterling sat up. "I don't suppose you could forget you saw us in bed together?"

"That wouldn't be fair to the community. Everyone has been worrying about you Sterling and pitying Daisy. People need to know." She gave Daisy another glare before she left.

Daisy put her hands on her fiery cheeks. "Oh my. I hope they let you stay until you're healed. I'd best pack just in case." She hurried out of the room before he could comment. She didn't want to hear anything he had to say. It would just make leaving worse. She couldn't ask anyone to lend her money for a ticket home. They'd just laugh at her.

Well she'd always known where she'd end up. She'd be acceptable if the man was drunk and it was dark. It had been so long since she had felt pretty. She'd nearly forgotten what it was like to go anywhere without people backing off, making comments, or turning away.

A short while later, she stood looking at her bed. Her few things were packed. She might as well make Sterling breakfast before she was asked to leave. It was her fault. She shouldn't have gone into his room, but she had been so scared. Sondra said she was the one who knocked, but what about the bang right outside the bedroom? Oh, Sondra was wicked. Why had she just walked into the house this morning?

Daisy whipped up eggs with sliced ham and took a deep breath before she carried the tray in to Sterling. Her hands shook as she carried it. As quickly as she could she set it down on the bed and turned to return to the kitchen.

"Wait. Daisy, don't go." His voice was so gentle.

She swallowed hard and stopped. After a few deep breaths, she turned and gazed at him. "I shouldn't have come in here. I'm all packed and ready to go. I'm sure you'll still be cared for. I was just so scared last night. That doesn't matter now. Thank you for your kindness. I hope you heal quickly. I'm going home, you see." She was rambling.

"I thought you weren't wanted there."

She shrugged. "Here, there, what's the difference? I can stay in the line shack. I couldn't bear the thought of living in the tiny place before, but now I welcome it. I'll have my privacy. I hope everything works out with Bill. Take care."

She held her head high when she walked out of his room. She heard him calling her, but she couldn't go back in there. Her heart couldn't take any more.

After she picked up her bag, she left the house taking one last look at it before she hurried away. She couldn't walk by Sondra, so she walked in the other direction. If she kept walking, she should come across the town. There was a saloon there and… Well, she'd think about that later.

Before long, the day grew warmer and she could have kicked herself for not packing food or water. She knew better, but her mind hadn't exactly been very clear that morning. Of course, Sondra had spread the news of how she had discovered Sterling and Daisy that morning. But had she embellished her story? Daisy snorted. Of course she had. It would be impossible to look anyone from the ranch in the eye again.

So Sondra didn't like her but why go out of her way to be rid of her? It made no good sense. Daisy wasn't any kind of threat to Sondra. Why she had her own house and a husband, and she should feel grateful. Sometimes there was no pleasing people.

Without any sort of warning, Daisy was falling forward. She hit the ground hard, and her foot hurt. Figured she had walked right into a gopher hole. She touched her throbbing ankle and knew enough to determine it wasn't broken. She gritted her teeth as she got to her feet. Upon looking around, she spied a tree branch that would do as a crutch as she walked. At the rate, she was going she wouldn't make it to town until the next day.

Lord, you must think I'm a ninny. I'm always near tears more than everyone I know combined. I'm too busy feeling sorry for myself, and I'm just plain stupid. How I could have ever thought a man wanted to marry me, I just don't know. I believed because I wanted it to be true. Please guide me to town and then I'm not sure you'll want to hear from me again. I'll be sinning, and I don't think I'll be able to bring myself to pray again. I know you are always with me. All my kindnesses and good deeds will be wiped away tomorrow. Maybe it would be nobler to just starve, but I don't know if I'll be able to do that. I do ask you to look after Sterling. He's a good man. And watch over my brother. I should be livid with him, but he just wants to have a life and be happy. I'll be fine so don't worry about me. I'll miss our talks.

She hobbled along until the sun went down. She had left the woods about an hour ago. One part of her wished someone would come upon her and stop to help, and the other part wished no one would see her. She sat under an oak tree for the rest of the night. It hurt trying to sit and the bark of the tree was painful against her back. She'd be fine. It didn't matter much, anyway.

Later, a movement next to her roused her from sleep. Something warm was pressed against her side. She held her breath and slowly moved to look. A large, mangy dog lifted his head and sniffed the air between them. His fur was matted, and his floppy ears clung to the sides of his head. She had no idea what color he was.

She reached out a hand and gently scratched his ears. "I won't judge you if you don't judge the way I look." The dog whined and closed its eyes again. He didn't seem to want to hurt her, and he might offer some protection. She nodded off again.

She woke at first light. What a fool she'd been about everything. She should have just had someone drive her to town. She could have said she was taking the stagecoach. No one would know for a few days she was working at a saloon, and by then she'd be unacceptable to respectable people. If they kept her as one of the women in the dark room, they might not know for weeks.

Her heart hurt. Drat that Sondra! Why did people always assume? Sterling wasn't even attracted to her. Maybe she should try to go farther away so Sterling could maintain some respectability. How far away was the next town? A sigh slipped free. What did it matter anyway?

When she sat and looked around, the dog was still there.

He got to his feet and licked her face. She'd never had a dog before.

"I don't care what you look like. We're both misfits, I guess. I won't be able to keep you at the saloon, though." She stood, and her ankle hurt worse than before. Slowly, she bent and picked up her homemade crutch. "Sorry boy, I don't have any food."

He barked and stared at her.

She turned and walked toward town. She hoped she would get there soon. It was taking so much longer on foot than the ride out in the wagon. Her mouth was as dry as sand, and her stomach growled. Oh, why hadn't she just been content with the line shack? She hadn't been grateful for what she'd been offered and now… She shivered. Her life was about to take a most unpleasant turn.

She went on, one painful step at a time. At last, the town was in sight. She dragged her foot, wincing with the agony, but she had to get there. Union soldiers… Her stomach churned. Nothing good ever came of associating with them. But they took one look and turned away. There weren't many people she could see. Maybe she could talk to Shelly before she continued on to her destination.

It took most of her energy to make it down the wooden walk. The dog stayed by her side.

"I really should give you a name if you're going to hang around. How about Rufus? I like it." Rufus didn't show any reaction. She shrugged and started walking again. The Kingsman Restaurant was open. She sighed in relief.

It was tricky getting the door open and walking through it with the crutch. She sat at the same table where she'd sat last time. Shelly didn't seem to be around. Maybe she was in the kitchen.

"What'll ya have?" an older woman asked.

"Water please."

The waitress stared at her. "You don't have any money do you?"

Daisy's face heated. "No, I don't."

"I'm sorry but you must leave. We don't allow scroungers to sit here."

"Is Shelly here?"

"No, she won't be in until the noon meal. I'm sorry, but you have to leave."

Daisy nodded. It was a struggle to make it to her feet. She was just so thirsty. She slowly made it out of The Kingsman. The saloon had to be here somewhere. She peered one way and then the other and spotted it across the street, down a bit.

Closing her eyes, she tried to compose herself. She needed the job. Rufus was suddenly by her side. "Glad to see you, Rufus. I still have nothing for you to eat."

Tears stung her eyes as she crossed the street, barely able to lift her leg, cringing every time she put weight on her injured foot. After what seemed forever, she stepped up onto the walkway. The pain was extreme, but she had to ignore it. Just a bit more and she'd be there.

She came to a building that was noisy for that time of the day. Taking a deep breath, she walked through the swinging doors, Rufus following her.

"We don't allow dogs in here," the bartender called out.

"Which one is the dog?" a man seated at a table yelled.

It was so hard to pretend she hadn't heard. "Rufus, you'll have to go outside."

The dog left. He was a smart one.

Daisy continued on to the bar. The bartender cocked his brow as he stood in front of her. "Did you need something?"

"A job," she whispered. "A job," she said louder.

"Take a step back so I can see you."

She stepped back and the way his eyes roamed her body made her feel dirty.

"A cripple?"

"No, I stepped into a gopher hole." She heard a few snide laughs.

He shook his head. "I'm not sure you're what we're looking for. You a virgin?"

How she wished she could turn and run. "Yes."

"I'd have to check to be sure." He gave her a cold smile.

"How can you tell?" she asked.

The men behind her began hootin' and laughing.

"If you have to ask you probably are a virgin. I might be able to use you. I can't offer a permanent job. If you can't attract customers then I don't need you."

It wasn't working out as she hoped. "Where else could I work?"

"The railroad camps have whores who follow the workers. They'd probably be glad of any woman. That would be your best bet."

"How far away?"

"Thirty miles at least."

"Which direction?"

"North."

She nodded. "Thank you." She turned and limped out of the saloon. How humiliating. She wanted to curl up and die. She couldn't walk thirty miles without food or water. She couldn't stay in town either.

Rufus was waiting for her. "You're the only bright spot in my day." Looking up at the sky she determined which way was north. If she was dumb enough she'd walk right onto the ranch. She need to go east for a while and then north to avoid them. Cautiously, she stepped down onto the dirt and walked. She either end up at the camp or dead. It didn't much matter to her.

CHAPTER SIX

"What do you mean you can't find her? She must have spent the night somewhere?" Sterling asked irritably. Where could Daisy be? If he could have, he would have stopped her. As it was, she had a good head start before Glory came to check on him. She instantly went to Parker, and a search party was formed.

Parker frowned. "I don't like it any more than you. No one has seen her. I'm thinking she must have made a camp last night. I hope we hear something soon. Why exactly did she leave?"

"Sondra," he said her name with distaste.

"What has she got to do with this?" Parker frowned.

"That night when everyone was on guard looking for Fletcher and Bill, Daisy got scared and came into my room. Then there was a knock on the door. She went toward it but no one called out for her to open it. We assumed it was Fletcher. She agreed to stay in this bed next to me so I could protect her. Then there was a loud bang against the outside of this wall. I told her to go to sleep and I'd keep watch." He took a deep breath. "Sondra must have a key because she let herself in and made accusations about the nature of the relationship between me and Daisy. She said she planned to tell everyone because she couldn't allow her respectable friends to be sullied by us. Well she talked as though she only meant Daisy. She tried her best and shamed Daisy."

Sterling clenched his jaw as he rubbed the back of her neck. "Nothing happened. Daisy is an innocent and would never…"

"I know. Did she say where she might go?" Parker asked. His expression had been one of concern, but as Sterling talked, it had grown angry, and now it was thunderous.

"She said she was going home." Sterling shook his head sadly. "Parker, she doesn't have a penny. How would she buy a ticket? No one will help her. She's a sweet woman, but people see the marks on her face and turn from her. Fletcher gave her so much hope when he asked her to marry him. But then he pulled her dreams out from under her. She took good care of me and never once complained. Most people on the ranch had been kind to her and she seemed to blossom right before my eyes." He sighed heavily. Never in his life had he felt so helpless. "Now I don't know. I fear she'll find trouble."

"Fletcher was cruel in how he treated her," Parker agreed. "We'll keep looking for her. Did she at least take provisions with her?"

"I don't know, but I don't think she took much if she did. She was too upset to think straight." He frowned. "What's wrong with Sondra?"

"I don't know. She plays up to Georgie and gets into her good graces and then she does something like this. It's not the first time. I'm sure Georgie will have something to say to her. Letty will be here soon to make you a meal. Do you need anything in the meantime?"

"No." Sterling sighed again. He needed to talk to Daisy

and tell her that not everyone saw just her face when they looked at her. She needed to know that no one would believe Sondra. And he might never get a chance to tell her.

The door close as Parker left. The house was so quiet. No footsteps, no rustling of her skirts as she worked about the house. And worst of all, no humming.

Lord, please watch over Daisy. People haven't been particularly nice to her. Others judge her for a few scars on her face. It's not right, and it hurts her. I know I'll have a limp when I heal and there will be stares. People will probably have something to say about it. I'm grateful I still have both legs, but Lord it's different for Daisy. She's so giving and no one tells her so or thanks her. I should have told her how beautiful she really was. Somehow, I thought she'd take it the wrong way. Please watch over her, and lead the men so they find her soon.

How could he have said she was beautiful without her denying it and getting mad? If he said she was beautiful on the inside it would sound as though she wasn't beautiful on the outside. She'd been told enough times she was ugly that she could see it in people's eyes. Hers was a hard burden to carry. Most of the women on the ranch had tried to make her feel welcome, and she had been starting to relax. She'd even smiled. Her singing was lovely. How he missed her. Where was she?

DAISY AND RUFUS were thrilled to have found a bit of water still in a puddle that hadn't dried up yet. They both drank their fill. It was getting dark, and she needed to find a place to bed down for the night. She'd lived a lot of her life outdoors, so she knew what to do. Her stomach rumbled. First, she would need food. She got busy making a few snares and hoped for a rabbit.

She placed three snares and then cleaned off a part of the ground for her to sleep on. Next, she gathered wood. If she managed to trap a rabbit, she'd need to cook it. The fire would also keep animals away. But it could also let people know where she was.

"What do you think, Rufus? Fire or no fire?"

Without warning, Rufus ran off, scrambling into the bushes. He came back in short order carrying a squirming rabbit in his mouth. He killed it and set in down in front of her.

Daisy stared, amazed. Then she chuckled. "That's the nicest gift anyone has ever given me. Fire it is." She was adept at skinning and cooking rabbit. Outdoor fires were a must to wash clothes, and she easily got one going. Tomorrow, she'd need water.

She cooked the rabbit, ate her half and gave Rufus his. But afterward, she wasn't feeling very well. Was it the rabbit?

A shiver chased a chill over her skin. Why hadn't she had brought a blanket? She needed to think before she allowed her emotions to drive her decisions. Perspiration formed on her forehead and Rufus looked listless. Oh no, they were probably getting sick.

Daisy lay down on the ground and tried to sleep, but her stomach hurt. She didn't know the cure. Her mother had given them witch hazel for most ailments. She suffered through the night, and at first light, she grabbed her crutch and pulled herself up. Her ankle still hurt but not as bad as her stomach. Painful cramps had started. Rufus didn't look energetic at all. He could barely raise his head, though his tailed thumped the ground in a half-hearted greeting.

She needed to find water and food and ride out whatever had made her sick. A cabin loomed in the distance, and she approached it. The place looked rundown, and the door was propped up. After pushing the door aside, she doubled over.

She made it to the outhouse. Tears poured down her face. She must have dysentery. When she was done, she threw the bucket down the well and then brought it up full or water. She poured that water into another bucket, splashing about half on the ground.

Rufus wasn't with her. Where had he gone? Was he even alive? The bucket was so very heavy. She set it near the bed in the dusty cabin. Next, she took a battered cooking pot she found in the kitchen area and limped out to pick as many berries as she could before she was bedridden. There were many raspberry bushes near the house. She filled the pot and hoped she would make it back to the cabin.

She pushed a chair next to the unmade bed and put the water and the berries on the it, and then found a tin cup for her to drink from. Doubling over in pain again, she screamed her agony. It was almost impossible to stay standing. She turned the raggedy sheets over and grabbed the blankets. They were coated in dust and grime, but they were better than nothing. When she finished, she fell into bed, making sure her crutch was within reach.

Her skin was so hot, so boiling but she kept the blankets on. Chills would start soon enough, if she did in fact have dysentery. She managed to get a cup of water and drink it down. Then she ate a handful of berries. Soon she might not be able to help herself and she needed to keep hydrated.

Lord, please help me. This pain is excruciating. I don't know if I'm meant to live or die, but I have faith in your path for me. I'm grateful I can't infect anyone else.

Another cramp gripped her, and she screamed again. And then she knew no more.

ANOTHER NIGHT WENT by and still no sign of Daisy. She

hadn't gone to town so where was she? Sterling pounded his fist on the bed. She could be in all kinds of trouble. If he could walk…

He glanced up and gritted his teeth. Sondra stood there watching him. She had a smirk on her face.

"You can leave," he growled.

"No, I can't. With so many looking for that Daisy we're shorthanded, and I'm the only one free to take care of you. I volunteered. Plus I need to thank you for telling Parker this is my fault. People who tell lies get theirs in the end."

He was dealing with a demented woman. "How's Green?"

"Walter is just fine. We have the perfect marriage. I do what I want, not like the other simpering wives who need permission for every little thing. Walter knows not to say no to me. It's a wonderful arrangement. I have a house, though I wanted it to be bigger than the other houses. Not bigger than Georgie and Parker's of course. We'll add on and I'll have my own garden. I know how the women feel about me. Well all except for Georgie. She can forgive anything."

"You should be ashamed of how you spoke to Daisy!" he practically shouted.

"Now we can't have you being so loud. I only spoke the truth. That's why I'm still living here. I may cause a bit of excitement but it's always truthful. You can't convince me you and Daisy in bed together was innocent. I'm not a fool, and I know how men are and how need driven they all are. I do feel bad for you, though."

He glared. "Why's that?"

"It must have been hard to have someone so ugly in your arms. Did you keep your eyes closed or was it dark? I did you a favor, you know. If she was still here, she'd expect more, and not only in the dark. She probably had plans to marry you all along. Fletcher had a near miss. He would have been miserable with a wife he couldn't look at without having a bad chill go through him."

"I don't need your help. You can go."

Sondra laughed. "You're not in charge here. I am. Has Daisy been seeing to your every need? Did she enjoy bathing you?"

"Get out! She has the morals of an innocent. You're just a hellcat! I bet you go to church every Sunday but you're in need of begging God's forgiveness for all you've done. Do you even know Daisy? Have you taken the time to find out what type of person she is?" He shook his head in disgust. "If you knew me, you'd know I'd never take an innocent to my bed. But you think you know all about us. Daisy has scars from smallpox. She ended up with the sickness because she was one of a few who took care of the town when many of the people came down with it. She is a sweet woman who wants a husband and children like many women do. And she finally thought she found someone to accept her, and he left her standing in town. Can you imagine how she must have felt? It was probably the most hurtful thing that ever happened to her. I can't stand for people to pretend to live in God's love on Sunday but the rest of the week they are just plain mean. I've seen a lot in my life but I've never seen the likes of you before. Banging on the bedroom wall to scare us, who in their right mind would do something like that? What if I had shot through the wall?"

Blotches of crimson dotted Sondra's cheeks, but she held her tongue.

Sterling's throat hurt from yelling. He reached for his cup and drank down some water. He set the cup back down with a heavy thump. "If you're here to help, then get on with it. There is probably more than enough cooking and cleaning to do to keep you busy."

Her eyes widened then they narrowed as she glared at

him. Without uttering a word, she turned and walked out of his room.

Sterling sat back against his pillow. That woman drained him, and he'd had about all he could take for one day. Where was Daisy? He needed her.

His brows shot up. He needed her? Did he have feelings for her? It was just concern, wasn't it? He wished he had his Bible with him. But one of Bill's men had used it to start a fire. He'd ask one of the other women if the preacher could stop by to see him.

HER DREAMS SCARED HER. In each, she was running away from someone. After a few tries she was able to use her cup to get water out of the bucket. She drank it right down. The painful cramping had gotten worse. Maybe help would arrive but she didn't have much hope. She forced herself to eat more berries. So many people died of dysentery, but she didn't plan to be one. She had beaten smallpox, she could beat this. She wished she had fresh sheets to put on the bed. It smelled like sickness in the cabin but there was no help for it.

No one would come. She had stumbled upon this cabin and doubted anyone lived here. It had looked deserted.

"So hot. So hot." Was that her voice? Why was it so dark out? Her confusion continued. What was real? Water, she needed to keep drinking water.

A while later she awoke again. Did I drink water last time? She reached for her cup, it was empty. She was so tired. Rolling she dipped the cup into water. If she could lift the bucket and pour it on her, she would be cooler. Drink, drink, drink. She only spilled half the water out of the cup. A painful cramp radiated through her body. She had to rest for a moment before she drank the water. She grabbed a handful of berries. Would she die here alone? They'd never know what happened to her. There were only a few who would care.

How long had she been here? She unbuttoned her dress and breathed easier. But she was beyond uncomfortable. Her clothes were soiled through. It was an exhausting fight, but she got her dress off and threw it on the floor. The door was still open. Would the smell of death bring predators? It was painful, oh so painful.

Please, Lord, stop this agony! If you're calling me home, sooner rather than later would be just fine.

She dreamed of her brother. They were running in the woods laughing and playing. Then they were in the family home and he told her girls didn't want to look at her. She put her hands to her face. All she felt was her bare skull. She screamed. She heard taunts, *you're ugly, hide away, shop later in the day so the good customers don't see you. Sorry but you can't eat here. You couldn't pay me to court her.* Her mind whirled. *Put her in a cage and charge money to see her. She's a circus animal.*

She was back at the schoolhouse bathing people's brows with a cold, wet cloth. *Bless you for taking care of us. You've always been so kind. Why isn't anyone else here to help? Bless you.* She ran from one sick person to the next and they were all dead.

She walked out of the schoolhouse into the glaring sun. Putting her arm up, she shielded her eyes. *You killed them. All dead because of you. How could you be so careless? This is your fault!* Fingers continued to poke her as she tried to leave but as soon as she thought she was at the end, she was instantly at the beginning again. *I'll never forgive you. Why didn't you save them? Why? Why? Why? You are the devil! You and the devil killed our families.*

Her brother walked to her, and she was relieved. "Here is

your new home." He showed her the line shack with a big cage on the inside. "You can't be around decent people ever again. No one wants you." He laughed at her.

Please, please no!!

She opened her eyes. A dreadful fright filled her. Glancing around, there wasn't a cage in sight. She took her petticoat off and found a clean place on it, which she ripped into smaller pieces. She reached over and put the cloth into the water and put it on her forehead. It was light out. How long had she been here?

A growl came from near the door. She turned her head, and it was Rufus warning off a raccoon. *Good, he's alive.* "I was worried about you, Rufus."

He turned his head and barked. For some reason he brought her peace. She took stock of herself. Her head didn't throb as much. Did this mean she was getting well or was it a signal that the end was near? If she closed her eyes again, would she be with the devil?

It took a long time, but she got her clothes off. She wrapped the sheet around her body. She needed to bathe; the smell of death still enshrouded her. Swinging her legs onto the floor, she wondered if she could grab a shirt she spotted hanging near the door. Maybe she could use her crutch to knock it off the peg. It took many tries, and she'd fallen asleep a few times but she finally got it and put it on. She'd do without sheets.

Once she woke, her dirty clothes were gone. Had she thrown them outside? She must have. That was the only possible explanation. Where was Rufus?

PARKER, Sandler, Max, Ross, and Willis all sat in the house.

Sterling was taking the smallest of steps, but he was grateful he made it to a chair in the sitting room.

"Has there been any rumor at all? Someone must have seen her by now." Parker scowled and shook his head.

"She made it to town," Willis said. "She stopped at The Kingsman restaurant but the waitress sent her on her way. Daisy didn't have any water, and she was using a crutch to get around."

"We should check with the doc," Sandler suggested.

"I already did," Max told them. "He never saw her, and then I went back and asked about the crutch, the waitress said it was a tree branch."

"She couldn't have gotten far from town," Ross commented.

Veronica walked into the house. "She asked for a job at the saloon. The bartender suggested she go north to the railroad camps."

Max stood. "You went into the saloon?"

She scrunched her nose. "Of course not. I talked to Carlotta, a woman who works there. She told me."

"And just how do you know Carlotta?" Max crossed her arms in front of him and stared at his wife.

Veronica gazed down at the floor. "If you must know, I give her a few baby things here and there. She had a baby a month ago. She doesn't know what she will do, but no one wants the baby staying there."

Max sighed in relief. "My wife the good-doer. It's nice you're helping."

"That's the best information we've had. Thank you, Veronica," Sterling said.

She nodded. "Best get back to the tea. I'm hosting it but I thought you needed to know. Take care, Sterling." She walked to the door. "See you later, Max," she tossed over her shoulder.

Sterling closed his eyes. A camp follower? He shuddered. Men didn't have a care how they used women in the camps.

"I'm glad we're between horse contracts. I think we could all split up and head north. One of us is bound to find her," Parker said.

"I hope she didn't go to the camp," Sandler said. Everyone nodded they all knew what went on in the tent camps.

"Where's Walter been?" Sterling asked.

"He's henpecked. Sondra has him working on the house." Parker said.

"I thought the house was new?" Sterling said.

Parker nodded. "I'm not sure how to handle it. Sondra seems to think now she has a house she can do whatever she wants. She's made more than one of the wives cry. Georgie is at her wits end, and she was the only one who tolerated her. I'm not happy Walter isn't pulling his weight around here. Building shelves or whatever he's doing doesn't benefit the ranch one bit."

"She gave me more than an earful why Daisy shouldn't be here," Sterling commented in disgust.

"Daisy is a sweet woman. She's helped with others' laundry, is great with children and offers to watch them and she gets taken up on her offer. She was even chopping wood and leaving some at each house here in Joy. She helped with homework and her farming background was put to use at the community garden. She'd enlarged everyone's gardens and gave each instruction on how to care for the plants. If you look, you'll notice that Veronica has flowers in front of her house and they've lasted more than a week. She never asks for anything in return. She blushes when anyone thanks her."

Sterling sat back in his chair. He had no idea Daisy had been doing anything besides taking care of him. She'd never once told him of her helpfulness or complained of being tired. People who judged her by her face were missing out on a rare jewel. His heart hurt. She could be in real trouble.

"Let's get going," Parker said. "Sorry you'll be sitting this one out," he told Sterling.

"I know your men will find her."

CHAPTER SEVEN

*D*aisy's body wouldn't stop shaking. She was chilled throughout. Rufus came away from the door and got on the bed and lay next to her. He was trying to help her stay warm. What a smart dog. She didn't know if she could hang on. She was weaker than she'd ever been. She only had a bit of water left, but she had plenty of berries.

Her life had been a series of ups and down. Growing up, she used to have a lot of fun with her brother. They'd climb trees, explore the woods, and go fishing. She had been sixteen when boys were looking her way, but her brother told her she was too young yet to receive gentlemen callers. She'd been happy, always the first to volunteer to help. If anyone was ill, she'd stay at their house and get all the work done plus take care of the patient under the advice of a doctor. Many smiled and waved at her when she went to town.

Then the smallpox came. They never found out how it started or who had it first. Daisy was on the farm and didn't hear about it until many had already died. No one would tend the sick people except for Doctor Dunn. Against her brother's wishes, Daisy went into town and walked into the schoolhouse where they had quarantined the people who had contracted the disease.

Her brother implored her to come home. He had stood outside the school pleading. But she couldn't leave. These were her neighbors, and frankly she was disappointed in the townspeople who didn't help. Some left food and water by the door. Others brought blankets and night clothes. A few held vigil waiting for any news.

The first she saw die had been a nice neighbor lady, and no one would remove her body. Daisy and the doctor struggled to put her outside, and there she lay, unclaimed. One day, Daisy took a shovel and dug graves, glaring at the men who watched her. They should be the ones digging. She had to drag the body herself and put the lady in one of the graves she had dug. She didn't have enough energy to cover the body with dirt.

There were two more that died the next day, and when she and Dr. Dunn carried out the bodies, they set then in the graves. The first grave stood uncovered by dirt. The people she'd been friends with disgusted her.

The schoolhouse was at full capacity and she wore herself out trying to help everyone. Dr. Dunn collapsed one day, and he died so fast she didn't have a chance to breathe. She was the lone caregiver to twenty people. Exhausted, she continued on. A few people pulled through, but they were the exception. Still more people came and they were getting fewer supplies. Even less water.

One day she stood on the front porch and begged for more water and more broth to feed those who could eat. She did get more water but no broth. She couldn't understand why people acted the way they had. Their loved ones were inside.

Then it happened. She collapsed, and no one was there to

help her. There were only seven survivors and folks blamed it on her. They didn't seem to remember how many died while the doctor was still alive. She lived, but she was marked for life.

She'd always been generous. If someone didn't bring a noon meal with them to school, she always shared hers. She helped younger students with their homework. She cooked meals for families who were in tight situations. The list was too long. All her good deeds were for naught.

When she was well, she walked out of the schoolhouse and went home. People expected her to stay and help their family members. It was all too much for her and she stayed on the farm for six months after that.

She went into town and the reception she got was freezing. It wasn't what she expected, and it devastated her. People pointed at her face and laughed. They whispered to each other, and when she went into the general store to buy sugar and coffee, the store owner pretended he didn't see her. He allowed every other customer to go before her. Her face heated the whole time she stood there in humiliation. Women put their noses in the air as they passed her. Finally, she left the store and went home empty handed.

She told her brother Dale, but he didn't act surprised.

"Things are different now. I'm sorry for it, but no man will ever want you and women judge others by how they look and what they wear. I'll go to town from now on."

That night she cried herself to sleep. It was so awful, but she'd learned her lesson and didn't go into town. She didn't even meet Dale's intended until a month before they were to be married. Daisy would never forget the look of horror in Kimberly's eyes. They ripped her heart out when she overheard Kimberly telling Dale she refused to have Daisy eat with them and it would be best if Daisy went to live elsewhere.

Why did people have to be so cruel? Whatever happened to love thy neighbor?

She reached and drank more water. She didn't remember seeing any expression, good or bad when she first met Sterling. If she was pretty, she would have hinted that she wanted him to court her. Who was she kidding she never had that much confidence but when you're dreaming it's nice to pretend.

She looked around and discovered supplies on the shelves. How had she missed this? She would have sworn the cabin was deserted when she stumbled on it. Who lived here and when would they be back? A chill raced through her.

STERLING WANTED TO THROW SOMETHING. There hadn't been a sighting of Daisy. What if she got lost or met up with a bear? He opened the door and with great effort, he walked onto the porch. He grabbed the nearest chair and slowly sat down. His legs shook, and he felt perspiration on his face and neck. He over did it, but he pushed harder than ever. He needed to find out what had happened to Daisy.

The scent of the fir trees refreshed him. He shook his head. Sondra was walking his way. He waited until she got to the porch steps.

"Don't take another step." He made his voice as cold as he could.

"I just wanted—"

"No. Go home. I never want you to darken any door of mine again." He glared at her.

Her eyes widened. "Why does everyone like her? Tell me that. No one seeks me out to talk."

Her whining grated him. "I'm not in the mood to insult you. I want you away from here."

He hadn't realized how loud his voice had gotten. Out of the corner of his eye, he saw Letty running his way. He relaxed.

"Sondra, it's my turn to check on Sterling." Letty turned to him. "Sorry I'm late."

"I'm grateful you're here," he responded. "Sondra was just leaving."

Sondra gave a loud, "humph," and walked away.

"It sounded like you didn't have any patience left for her."

"She's not my favorite person."

Letty stepped up to the porch and sat in the chair next to him. "No word?"

"None. I wish she had stayed. If Sondra wanted to tell the whole town, we were in bed together, I would have married Daisy."

Letty smiled. "In bed with you? Things look a mite different now," she teased.

"She was frantic. Sondra pounded on our door that evening and then there was a bang against the outside of the house where my room is. Sondra admitted that she did it. She's got everything she wanted. She has Walter and a nice house."

"Sometimes things don't matter. She is jealous of anyone Georgie spends time with. She's been nasty to just about every woman on this ranch. I heard her once complain that tea was supposed to be just her and Georgie. She needs to open her eyes and see it ain't that way anymore. Life is about adapting to each change and the good Lord is always changing things. Some changes are good some, aren't but you have to go with what you got."

He nodded. "It's no excuse."

"I didn't mean it to be one. You look worn out. Are you sure you should have walked this far so soon?"

"No. I'm not sure, to tell you the truth. I'd give anything

to be able to search for Daisy. I'm worried sick. She has it in her mind she has no worth. Someone should have taken a horse whip to the people in her town, then to her brother, Fletcher next, and finally Sondra. Each made her feel worthless because of her scars. She is so much more. Don't they see the kindness and generosity or the love inside of her?"

Letty grinned. "I think as long as you see those things it'll be just fine."

"Not if she's not found."

"Do you need me to help you back to bed?"

He shook his head. "I could use a cup of water, please."

"I'll be right back."

Lord, please let Daisy be all right. Help us find her. I won't interfere with the law catching up to my brother again. I thought it right at the time, but now I realize how wrong I've been. When people rob and hurt others, they should face the law. Daisy has gotten into my heart, Lord, and I want her to know her worth. I wish people were kinder. Thankfully, not all people judge others.

Letty came back outside and handed him a cup of water. "I need to get home and make supper. I'll bring you some soon." She gave his shoulder a light squeeze before she left.

DAISY STIFFENED when she heard voices outside.

"Gabriel, I'm beginning to think my mother isn't in this area after all. What is that smell?" It was a women's voice. Daisy tightened her grip on the blanket.

"Lydia, we'll find her," a man said.

Rufus dived off the bed, barking noisily.

"Rufus come back!" Would they hurt the dog?

A dark-skinned man came through the door, rifle in hand. "Who are you?" He put his arm across his nose.

84

"Dysentery, I don't know if you can catch it or not," she warned.

The man backed away. "It's a catching sickness."

"I think I'm over the worst of it," she tried to shout, but her throat was hoarse.

A woman with a cloth pressed against her nose and mouth stepped into the cabin and stopped. "I'm Lydia and that was my husband Gabriel. How long have you been sick?"

"I don't know, at least three days. I've been in and out. I thought no one lived here."

"We've been staying here for a bit. Who can I tell to come get you?" Lydia asked.

"I'll just be on my way. Let me drink more water and I'm sure I'll be strong enough to continue on." Even as she said the words, she knew she didn't have strength enough to walk across the cabin.

"I'm going to open the window. We'll fetch some fresh water then I will heat water in the hip bath for you. You won't be going anywhere for a few days. Are the clothes out here the only ones you have?"

Daisy nodded.

"We'll boil them real good. You survived, and that is a miracle. We'll get this place scrubbed down so we're all safe."

Daisy thanked the woman. Her eyes were darker than her husband's and they held much kindness.

Lydia was a bit bossy, but she got things done. Daisy was soon washing herself in the tub while all items including the blankets were boiling in a big tub outside. Being clean had never felt so good. Lydia gave her men's clothing to wear. They'd been in a trunk Daisy'd never looked in.

They even removed the bed. When Daisy was dressed, she sat on the floor with her back against the wall. She was so tired.

"Here, try to drink more water," Lydia coaxed as she put

the rim of the cup against Daisy's lips. She drank and then felt herself being laid down. Her head landed upon something soft, and they covered her with a cloak. She slept.

Later she woke and Gabriel was trying to spoon broth into her mouth.

"I'm so sorry you had to come home to find this mess."

"Where were you going before all this happened?"

"I thought I'd try to find a job at one of the railroad camps."

Gabriel's eyes widened. "Do you understand what job you would have found there?"

Daisy nodded. "I have nowhere to go, and people can't stand to look at me."

Lydia turned from the stove. "Why?"

"Please don't tease me. I've heard how ugly I am for a long time now."

Lydia came to her and squatted down next to her husband. "You haven't been around the right people. I hardly know you, but I know you're a good person. That should be enough. But I know," she gestured to Gabriel. "We know how it is to be judged before we utter one word. We had to leave the last place we worked, so I thought I'd look for my mother. People told me all my life she was at one plantation around Sweet Water. But many of them are deserted."

Daisy felt more at ease than she had in a very long time.

THE NEXT DAY Daisy was able to walk about a bit. She'd leave the young couple soon. She stood in front of the stove while both Lydia and Gabriel were outside. The pounding of horses' hooves filtered in through the door, and she feared trouble was out there.

Picking up the rifle, she grabbed a few shells and loaded it. Next, she tiptoed to the side of the door so she could peek out. Her heart skipped a beat and she thought for sure she was seeing things. Fletcher and a man who she assumed was Bill were off their horses. Bill grabbed Lydia while Fletcher aimed his gun at Gabriel.

Daisy'd never used a rifle before, but she had watched her brother enough times she knew how it was done. She stepped out into the middle of the entry and cocked the rifle. Fletcher turned, saw her, grinned, and aimed. Before he shot her, she'd pulled the trigger and almost landed on her backside.

For a moment, she wasn't sure if she was all right. Gabriel snatched up Fletchers gun and pointed it at Bill.

"Get your hands off my wife!"

"I'm not the bad one. You already shot the outlaw. I'm glad you did. He kept threatening me if I tried to leave him." Bill pushed Lydia to the ground and pulled his gun out of his holster but Gabriel was faster. Bill went down with a look of surprise on his face.

"They'll hang us if they find out," Lydia screamed. "Gabriel, what are we going to do?"

Daisy got her footing and stepped outside. "Fletcher, the one I shot planned to make me... Well he had the whole ranch on extra guard. That other one is Bill. He's an actual outlaw. He robs banks, raids farms, and kills people. I was nursing his brother before I left the ranch."

"We have to run!" Lydia urged. She dashed inside and threw things into a sack.

"Wait! If you help me bury them, I'll say I killed them both. I'll say you weren't even here. I can't go back and tell Sterling I left his brother to rot." She glanced around for Rufus, but he was nowhere in sight. Hopefully he was still alive.

"I don't know..." Lydia started.

"Tell me about this ranch while I dig. I'm only burying the one," Gabriel said before he rolled up his shirt sleeves.

"STERLING, I hate to say it, but we need to call off the search. It's been over a week," Parker said as he stood in the kitchen, hat in hand.

Sterling nodded. "I figured as much. She's probably at one of those camps by now."

"Not from what I heard, at least not the nearest one. I asked around and, do you remember Milkins? He's in charge of the camp. I sent a telegram, and they haven't seen her."

"Someone put Milkins in charge?" Sterling laughed and Parker joined him.

"He didn't even know how to put his shoes on right when he enlisted," Sterling added.

"At least we know where she isn't." Parker said and all laughter stopped. "I wish I had some answers for you. I really do."

"I know you do, Parker. All we can do now is pray."

Parker nodded. "I'll have the preacher say an extra prayer for her on Sunday. I have lots of work to do. Can't wait until you're all healed up and working. You are planning to stay aren't you?"

"I've given it a lot of thought. I don't owe Bill a thing. I saved his bacon more than once. I'm done with that life."

"Glad to hear it. I'll try to stop by later." Parker left.

It was quiet, too quiet in the house. He missed Daisy humming and singing. He missed her cooking and her smiles. She had to be out there somewhere. He refused to think of her as dead.

CHAPTER EIGHT

"I still don't think we should show up with these horses," Gabriel said a few days later.

"I'm just returning the horse to Bill's next of kin. Least ways that's the way I'm thinking of it," Daisy said. She rode Bill's Chestnut gelding while Fletcher's Bay carried all their supplies. She was weak, and her ankle still pained her, and she couldn't walk very well; they decided not to take chances with the healing process.

"It looks as though a storm is blowing in," Lydia said as she looked at the sky.

"We'll be on the ranch soon," Daisy told them. She spotted a line shack she had passed when she'd left. It was a little bigger than an outhouse but she might not have much choice. Would Dale even send her money to get back home? Her shoulders sagged. She doubted it. There still had been no sign of Rufus and she feared the worst. He was a good dog.

They continued on and were approached by a mixture of freedmen and white cowboys. Lydia and Gabriel frowned as they exchanged glances.

"It's just extra patrols to keep everyone safe," Daisy said.

"You're Daisy aren't you?" a cowboy asked.

"That's Daisy," Darrius confirmed with a wide smile.

"It's so good to see you, Darrius. I feel like I've been gone forever."

"They called off the search a few days ago," he revealed, shaking his head. "I sure am glad you're safe. Who are these two?"

"This is Lydia and Gabriel. They helped me get well and then they brought me here."

Two of the cowhands got off their horses and offered them to the young couple.

"It's fine," Daisy encouraged her new friends.

Gabriel helped Lydia get on one horse and then mounted the other.

"Daisy, you have a bunch of people worrying about you," said Darrius. "They'll be happy to see you. Letty's been moping around since you left."

"You work here?" Lydia asked Darrius.

"I sure do, and my family lives on the ranch too." He smiled at Lydia. "You folks need a place to stay?"

"Maybe if Parker lets me stay on the ranch, they can stay with me. If there isn't room somewhere else, that is. Women in one bedroom and the men in the other?" Daisy suggested.

"I'm sure Parker will figure something out," Darrius replied. "Right now, I know of someone who needs to see you. Sterling's been worried out of his mind about you."

Sterling had been worried? Stunned, Daisy nodded and they urged their horses to follow the cowboys. Her heart pounded. What would Sterling say? *No one makes coffee as well as you? I hate waking up to an empty house?* He probably *was* somewhat worried but not to the extent Darrius suggested. Had Sterling made much progress with his leg?

She held on tight, afraid of slipping off. Her energy was so depleted.

Without saying a word, Darrius plucked her from her saddle and set her in front of him.

"Thank you." She leaned against him and fell asleep.

***

STERLING THOUGHT he was seeing things. That was Daisy sitting in front of Darrius, wasn't it? He didn't recognize the other two. The horses seemed to be moving so slow in coming closer. Finally, they all reined in. One man got down and took Daisy into his arms until Darius got down. Then Darrius took her back into his arms. He smiled at Sterling.

"I think you've been looking for this one."

Sterling smiled, but when he saw how gaunt Daisy looked, his happy expression became a frown. The circles under her eyes spoke of trouble. "Can you put her on her bed?"

Darrius carried her inside, and Sterling turned to the newcomers. "Thank you for bringing her home. I'm Sterling."

"I'm Gabriel and this is my wife Lydia. We found her in a cabin we'd been using. We'd been gone for a while looking for my wife's mother."

Sterling nodded his understanding. "No luck?" he assumed, since there was no sign of another woman.

"Nothing so far," Lydia told him.

There was something about the way Lydia stood that reminded him of someone. He shook his head to clear his thoughts. It would come to him. "Come on in."

Sterling slowly stepped into the house and down the hall to the bedroom. Daisy hadn't woken, and his heart hurt looking at her.

"I'll see if Georgie can come. Letty and Glory are teaching school."

"Thanks, Darrius. I appreciate it." He didn't even look

away from Daisy when he spoke. He cautiously lowered himself onto the bed beside her.

"She's been sick," said Gabriel.

Tears stung Sterling's eyes, and he blinked them away.

"Dysentery she said, and I'm certain she was right. She's a survivor," Lydia offered. "I'll go get some cool water and a cloth."

Sterling nodded. He reached out and stroked Daisy's face with his fingers. She wasn't ugly, not at all. He could have lost her.

Gabriel and Lydia came back in, and Lydia handed Sterling a wet cloth, He bathed Daisy's face with it.

Georgie ran into the room almost out of breath. "Oh, my! What happened?"

"Georgie, this is Gabriel and his wife Lydia. They brought Daisy home."

"Thank you, thank you. Do you know what happened?"

Lydia told her the story of finding her and the dysentery. Sterling wasn't sure why but he knew she was leaving something out.

"If you men will excuse us I want to get Daisy into a nightgown and check her over." Georgie helped Sterling stand. "Don't overdo it. I don't need more patients."

"Yes, ma'am." He hobbled along with Gabriel walking right behind him. They sat at the kitchen table, and Gabriel poured them both coffee.

"What makes you think Lydia's mother is around these parts?"

"We talked to anyone who knew her, and they thought she'd never leave until she had her children with her. We've been to so many towns and not so warmly greeted. One person knew who she was but didn't know where she went."

"Did you have time to go into Sweet Water? There's a shanty town there and many leave messages for those they are looking for. There is a woman named Adele there who takes down the messages and asks around."

"No, we didn't get that far yet."

"Does Lydia have brothers or sisters?"

"She doesn't know. She'd been at the plantation since she was a baby. She'd been told her mother died but later someone told her the truth that she was sold days after she was born. I think if we don't find her soon we'll head out west."

"Your wife reminds me of someone. I just can't think of who, but I'll work on it. Georgie can ask her husband Parker to send someone with a message for Adele."

"You really have freedmen living and working like regular folk?" Gabriel shook his head. "I swear I must be seeing things."

Sterling smiled. "They work alongside the other cowhands. If they have other skills, that's a plus. This is one of the houses in Joy. The freedmen named this area Joy. It's on Parker's ranch. The children all go to school, and we all go to church together. It was Georgie's vision, I hear. She wanted the ranch to be a community."

"This house is for people who were slaves? Do they get paid or is the house and anything else taken from your wages until there is a big debt and you can never leave?"

"This is one of the few honest outfits. The only difference is some freedmen are new to rounding up cattle and horses, but Parker makes sure everyone learns and everyone is safe. It's a miracle. Parker told everyone if they can't live and work side by side with a freedman they could take their horse and leave. From what I hear, a few left. I haven't been here very long. I served under Parker in The War Between the States. I'd been trying to keep my brother Bill from getting killed."

Gabriel stilled. "We had a bit of trouble at the cabin. Daisy knew one of them. I think his name was Fletcher, and she said Bill was someone's brother."

"What happened? Where is Bill?" Sterling's heart pounded.

"I killed him." Gabriel whispered.

"What happened?" Sterling took a few deep breaths to keep calm.

"They rode up on us. The one named Bill grabbed Lydia while the one named Fletcher kept his gun trained on me. Daisy was inside and she came out with her rifle and shot Fletcher right out of his saddle. The other one still had Lydia. He tried to tell us he wasn't the outlaw and we'd saved him from Fletcher. Daisy didn't seem to believe him. I dived for the gun Fletcher'd dropped, and the man pushed Lydia while drawing on me. I got him before he got me. I'm sorry. Daisy made sure we buried your brother, but we didn't bother with that Fletcher fellow. As soon as it happened, I wanted to head west, but Daisy convinced us to take her here. Said no one would string us up."

"So, he finally reaped what he sowed." Sterling sighed, half in sorrow, half in relief. "It's just a shock to hear he's dead." He shook his head and met Gabriel's gaze. "No. No one will string you up. There are two less evil people in the world." He chuckled. "I didn't know Daisy could shoot."

Gabriel let out a soft laugh. "I don't think she did either."

Sterling nodded and stared into his coffee. A huge weight fell from his shoulders, though he felt guilty at his relief. He should be upset or wanting to punch Gabriel, but he didn't want to do either. He glanced up into Gabriel's haunted and scared expression.

"I don't bear you any bad will. My brother told me he got a bullet out of my leg, but he didn't. And when it turned to gangrene, he drove a wagon here, rolled me to the ground, and kept going. You don't do that to your brother. My mother made me promise to watch over Bill, and I tried, but I feel free of her promise now. It was so hard to keep it, and I should have just decided enough was enough and left a long time ago."

Parker joined them just as Sterling finished speaking. "Bill is dead?"

Sterling nodded. "Fletcher too."

"No offense, but it means we won't have to string them up ourselves. They would have been back," Parker said in a serious tone.

"I know," agreed Sterling. "Parker this is Gabriel. He and his wife Lydia brought Daisy home. She's been real sick."

Parker put his hand out to shake Gabriel's, and the look of surprise on Gabriel's face reminded Sterling that the country still had a long way to go. Gabriel shook Parker's hand.

Would there be peace in his lifetime? Would his children treat others as equals? Parker was making a good start here at the ranch, and he wanted to stay to be part of it. He shook his head in surprise. Children? He'd never thought about having a family before.

"Sterling?" Parker asked.

He pushed a smile onto his face. "Just doing some thinking is all. You don't suppose I could stay on here? With my obligation to Bill over I feel like a new person."

"I don't doubt it. It must have been a horrible burden to carry. You're lucky you're not in jail."

Sterling nodded. "I realize just how lucky I am."

Georgie and Lydia came out of the bedroom. Georgie smiled at Parker and went to his side. He easily put his arm around her waist and tugged her closer.

Parker studied Lydia. "She's the image—"

"—Of Letty's girl," Sterling finished for him.

Lydia's eyes widened, and Gabriel pulled out a chair for her. "Don't get your hopes up too high, Lydia."

"I know, Gabriel."

"You're looking for your mother?" asked Parker.

"I have been for a few years now, but we keep running into dead ends. We'll head west soon, I think, and start our lives," Lydia explained.

"I could go get Letty," Parker offered.

"Talking about me again? I hear Daisy—" Letty stared at Lydia. "Oh, my word." Her hands shook as she put one over her heart.

"Who's your people?" Letty's voice trembled.

"I'm looking for my mother. All I know is they took away me from her a few days after I was born. No one knew which plantation I came from, so I haven't found out anything."

"Your daddy wasn't with you?" Letty asked.

"No, ma'am."

"How about a man named Matthias?" Letty looked to be both eager and upset.

"He was always very kind to me and Gabriel."

"You and Matthias got to the plantation about the same time?"

"The same day, but he didn't know who my mother was."

Letty gasped and tears filled her eyes.

"I'll get Darrius," Parker said as he hustled out the door.

Lydia stood up and took a step toward Letty. "Gabriel?"

Gabriel stood next to her and held her hand. "I think you found your mother."

"Do you think's possible?" Lydia asked Letty.

"More than possible. Matthias was your father and I am your mother." Tears streamed down her face and she opened her arms wide. Lydia flew into them.

The whole room was filled with emotion. No one was dry eyed. Darrius barreled in and stared at his wife. "Is it true?"

Letty broke their embrace and took hold of Lydia's hand. "Take a good look at her."

"She's the image of our daughter Hannah. I was so worried about Daisy I hardly did more than glance. What's all this crying for? I think a celebration is in order."

Georgie hopped up. "I'll plan one for this evening." She gave Letty a kiss on her cheek as she passed her.

DAISY HEARD a commotion in the kitchen but the tone sounded happy so she didn't worry. She needed to tell Sterling about Bill. Bill's death sat heavy on her heart. She felt better than she had in over a week. Being in her night gown and her bed made such a difference.

She strained to listen, hoping to catch what everyone seemed happy about. Darrius was talking about a celebration. What was going on? A sigh slipped out. What did it matter? She was too tired to celebrate. Instead, she napped for a bit, and when she awoke it was quiet.

She turned over and there was Sterling sitting in a chair next to the bed. She gasped in surprise.

"Hello, Daisy," he said softly.

She might as well tell him and get it over with. "I saw your brother. He—"

Sterling reached and took her hand in his. "I already know. Don't look so sad. He wasn't a good man. I'd hate to think what he and Fletcher would have done to the three of you. More likely you'd all be dead, and I doubt it would have been an easy death. All I care about is that you're back."

"I made sure he was buried."

He kissed the back of her hand. "I know. Gabriel told me. I also know you almost died. The thought of you dying hurts my being. I'm so grateful to God that He brought you back."

Emotions rose, and a lump formed in Daisy's throat. She swallowed hard. "Did… did Sondra tell everyone I'm a whore? It preyed on my mind. Everyone had been so good to me, and the thought of them hearing horrible things about me was too much for me to bear."

"Is it true you think the only value you have is being a whore?" His voice was filled with kindness.

"In the dark." It didn't even make her tear up anymore. Fate was fate. "They wouldn't hire me in town. What do women who aren't good enough to be a whore do? The choices are none."

"You're thinking with Sondra's words. She doesn't speak for the rest of us. Everyone was upset when you left. People searched for you. I was scared for you. Dysentery and you're here to tell about it? They said you took care of yourself."

He cared for her? "I was foolish enough to leave without supplies. It was a daunting thing until I reached the cabin. I didn't have water, so I drank out of a puddle. I know better, but that was all I could find. I'm sorry I put everyone to so much trouble. I'm not worth making a fuss over."

"You think you're worthless? Daisy you are so much more than you think. You are the sweetest, most caring woman I know."

"It doesn't count for much. I've had to find out the hard way more than a few times before it stuck, and when I shot Fletcher it didn't feel good. I don't blame him for not claiming me; I blame him for threatening me." She lifted one shoulder and let it fall. "But he's gone…"

"I missed you. I missed your smile and your singing and talking with you."

She didn't believe him, but she said nothing.

"Lydia is Letty's daughter."

"Is it true?" Her heart lifted, and she smiled. "How exciting! I'm overjoyed for them. God works in mysterious ways, doesn't He? Was that what all the commotion was about? I can't wait to see them together! They are both such lovely women."

"Why don't you rest up and maybe we can watch the celebration from the front porch. That's as far as I can walk."

"You've made wonderful progress. You should be proud of yourself. I know I am. The first time I saw your leg I didn't have the highest hope you'd be able to use it."

He grimaced. "I'll probably have a limp."

"That doesn't matter. People like you, and there is still plenty you can do around the ranch."

He stared into her eyes. "People like you too. Remember that." He kissed her hand again before pushing up to a standing position. "We both need rest." He limped out slowly.

He meant well, but a limp was not the same as being ugly. She had never felt uncomfortable around Lydia or Gabriel. They had just accepted her without giving her a second look. Maybe there was some powder she could use to cover the marks on her face. No… It was no use. She'd used up her bravery coming to Spring Water. The stares she'd had to endure throughout the trip were horrendous, but she got through thinking she was getting married. But now… Not one thing was turning out the way she thought it would. She was still alive, thank God. Her inner strength was stronger than she would have ever thought.

And what a twist of fate that Letty and Lydia were mother and daughter. They must be in heaven to have found each other. She blinked her eyes. This house would belong to Lydia and Gabriel. That meant she'd need to move out soon. She'd need to telegraph Dale after all.

CHAPTER NINE

he fiddle played and people were dancing. It was a wonderful sight. Daisy felt warm and happy. Glory made sure both Daisy and Sterling were covered in blankets. All the women set up a mini buffet on the porch just for the two of them.

Letty hugged her so many times she lost count. Her happiness was contagious, and Daisy felt the happiness in her own heart.

"It's really a miracle that it was Letty's daughter who found me in her cabin. It was such a horrible mess, but she took charge and cleaned one area at a time making sure that she and Gabriel wouldn't catch what I had. She even readied a hot bath for me and boiled my clothes."

"Glory said it was a miracle you survived by yourself. How did you know to eat raspberries?"

"I didn't. There were bushes of them right next to the house, and I hadn't eaten. I knew it was a matter of hours before I'd be flat on my back so I made sure I had water to drink and berries to eat. God was looking out for me." She smiled.

"Yes He was." Sterling reached across the table and took her hand in his big, calloused warm one.

Her body tingled like it never had before. Was she still sick? But no, this felt different, like a reaction to his touch. She loved it when he touched her ever so lightly. Was she setting herself up for heartbreak? It was wrong, but if she had done the things Sondra accused her of at least she'd have that memory to get her through. Now she studied his profile and tried to commit everything to memory. Her brother had always been in a bad mood, but she hadn't such anger and foul tempers as he'd suffered here on the ranch. Most of the men were actually cheerful.

Why couldn't she just enjoy the moment? It was probably too much doubt and worry about her future. But one thing was for certain: she wouldn't be going to any of the railroad camps. Maybe she could build a house of her own, little by little. She'd have to have a garden. She didn't think Dale would remember to feed her. He had a few line shacks but she would take the one farthest away. Somehow she'd shore it up so it wouldn't be cold. It was surprising how bitter and frosty some nights could get. There was a stream near that piece of property. She'd be just fine.

"You look peaceful. What are you thinking about?"

"I was thinking I could take a bad situation and turn things around. Living in a line shack won't be so bad. I'm planning a garden for food, and there is a stream close by. Maybe I can scrounge and find wood to make the shack bigger. Oh, and I can fish. I'll bring some books with me, and I'll be fine. I left home because the thought of living in a shack was unbearable, but I didn't realize just how lucky I was. There will be no one to stare at me, no one to bear false witness against me. Maybe it'll heal my heart. And I won't bring a mirror." She smiled, hoping he thought her to be happy.

He stared at her, jaw slackened.

"Maybe I'll get a dog," she continued. "Did I tell you about Rufus? He was a mangy dog I came across, and he drank the same water as me. I didn't see him for a few days but then when I had the chills and was shaking he jumped onto the bed and the heat from him was amazing." A bit of sadness threatened to overcome her, and her smile faded. "I wish I knew what happened to him. He wasn't much to look at, but he made me feel better, safer."

"It sounds like you've done a lot of planning. It all sounds nice except you'll be alone."

"I think it for the best." She gave a resolute nod. "My heart is weary. I blamed others because they didn't like to look at me. The fault was mine. I should have just stayed home and not subjected others to the sight of my face. I can't change things. I can't make them remember that I took care of their loved ones or that I was first to volunteer to help others. It just hurts me, and the hurt piles up until I sometimes feel as though I can't breathe. I've been praying, and this is my solution."

He looked into her eyes and then his gaze explored her whole face. Finally, she turned her head as tears filled her eyes. Not Sterling too. Her heart fell with a thud.

"You two need anything?" Mary Beth asked as she stepped up onto the porch.

"Actually, I'm so tired. Could you make sure Sterling makes it inside? Thank you." She jumped up and hurried into her room and closed the door. She should be used to people staring by now, and to some extent she was. But it was Sterling. He had just seen every scar and every mark. She was surprised he hadn't turned away.

Now she could say she knew what it was to love, though. It was part wonderful and part agony. And one day Sterling would find himself a pretty wife, and they'd have adorable children. They'd attend church with the others, and the children would all play together. She didn't like to hold babies; it reminded her of what she wouldn't ever have.

Oh Lord, help me. I need to get home as soon as I can. Please let me find a way back.

SHE'D GOTTEN up early and headed to Georgie's. Perhaps all she'd been doing would be worth the price of a stage ticket. Georgie was sad she was leaving but happily gave her the money plus enough for food. She made arrangements to leave in an hour for town.

With a heavy heart, she walked into the house she shared with Sterling.

"You're up and you made coffee! You sure are on your way to a full recovery. I'm glad for you. I'm leaving for home. Finally, I'm going home. I wish I had time to visit with you but I need to pack." She swiftly went into her room and closed the door. She leaned against it and closed her eyes. It was going to be so hard to say goodbye to Sterling. But it was for the best.

She packed her meager belongings and was ready with time to spare. Gathering her courage, she walked into the kitchen, but Sterling wasn't there. His bedroom door was closed, and she went to knock on it but pulled her hand at the last moment. If he wanted to say good bye and good luck, he would have been waiting.

She picked up her bag and left.

HE WASN'T PREPARED to let her go. He had done her an injustice by hiding in his room, but she had so many plans for a new life. There wasn't room in it for him. She'd only come to Texas to marry Fletcher. Most brides probably would have gone home. He stood on the porch and watched as Noah drove the wagon with Daisy sitting straight and tall on the bench. She was taking a piece of his heart with her. As soon as she was out of sight, it was if a cloud covered the sun and stayed there.

Why hadn't he said anything? He closed his eyes against the ache in his chest. She probably wouldn't believe him anyway. They had gotten to be good friends, but he hadn't behaved like one when he had refused to say goodbye or ask her to write to him. She felt something when he touched her. He'd seen it in her eyes last night. There was still time! He could saddle a horse and go after her. He slid down onto a chair, shaking his head. He'd never make it to town.

What did she see when she looked at him? Did she consider him damaged and possibly useless? Maybe she thought she'd have to spend her life taking care of *him*. One more person making demands of her, playing on her kind-hearted nature and asking her to do for him. Loneliness engulfed him, and only Daisy could take it away. After taking a deep breath, he let it out slowly. He needed to compose himself. He stood, went into the house and into her room. He found a hairpin on the wood plank floor. He had a hard time picking it up, but he managed. He grabbed her pillow and hobbled back to bed.

Her sweet scent was on the pillow and it made him feel worse. Why hadn't he said anything when she went on about a garden and maybe building on to the line shack herself? It was dangerous for a woman alone. It seemed to him that the shack was clear on the other end of the property.

He'd met plenty of women but none as selfless as Daisy. None that he wanted to marry. He'd get someone else to ride into town to get her and bring her back. He sung his legs off the bed and stood, gritting his teeth against the pain. He heard someone enter the house. Was it Daisy?

"Did you have any breakfast?" Georgie asked.

He sat back down on the bed. "I'm not hungry. I'm thinking maybe I could get someone to go into town and bring Daisy back."

Her brow furrowed. "She probably just made it to the stage on time. I don't think she's in town any longer. She left suddenly… Did you two have words?"

He shook his head. "She got it in her head she was shaming everyone by living here with me. And she thinks she's too ugly to look at. I didn't expect her to leave, though. I thought I had plenty of time. She just got back…" He ran his fingers through his thick hair. "Maybe she didn't want to be stuck with a man with a limp."

"Daisy doesn't judge people, and she wouldn't care if you limped. She only said that it was time for her to go home. I thought maybe she missed her brother." Georgie shook her head.

"Her brother doesn't want her. She gets to live in a line shack when she gets home." He wanted to hit something.

"Oh dear. What kind of brother is that? I shouldn't have given her the money to buy a ticket."

"Georgie, you couldn't have possibly known. She worked hard and deserved to be paid, but I should have paid her." He drew a shaky breath. "And I should have made her stay."

"I didn't know it was that way between you two. I know she admired you and I'd catch her looking at you a lot, but she never said a word to me. And there's no shame in nursing a man. She carries too much on her shoulders. I could send a telegram and ask her to come back."

Sterling sighed. "No, she wanted to leave. She mentioned last night she could have a garden and there was a stream nearby. I should have told her not to go, but I didn't think she'd actually go back there."

"I'm going to miss her," Georgie said with a sigh.

"Me too." He buried his face in his hands.

With a whisper of cloth, Georgie discreetly left.

Lord, watch over Daisy. She tries to pretend she doesn't care that people stare at her. I'm afraid she'll shut herself away. She should be the one walking the streets as an example of a good person. Can people not see what their meanness does? The world is not made up of perfect people. We all have flaws. Hers is just there for everyone to see. She's judged before she can even say hello. People know nothing about her yet they think she's not good enough. How much pain does she have to bear, Lord? My heart hurts, but her pain is much greater. Help me to heal so I can go after her.

He put her pillow under his head.

CHAPTER TEN

The sun was blazing. The one thing she wished she still possessed was her big bonnet, but a man had grabbed it off of her and wanted her to jump and retrieve it as he held it up over his head. She'd ignored him. She would need to get around to making another soon. But now she bent and, using an old tin can, she scooped water from her bucket and watered her plants. She was pleased with her garden; it should yield plenty for her to eat. She was getting sick of dandelions and fish. She snared a rabbit here and there, but she wanted be sure there were enough rabbits for winter.

If she walked far enough she'd come to a wagon train path, and there she always found many treasures. Yarn and a crochet hook, a few books, a nice chair that didn't fit in the line shack. It was nice for sitting outside and reading, though. She'd also found more ripped canvas. First, she covered the leaky roof with it then used the rest to cover her things that had to stay outside. She stumbled across a few cannon balls but left them. She carried the things to a place in the woods so she could get them later. It was a bit of a walk but worth it. Her kitchen now had a few utensils.

Dale yelled and lectured as soon as he saw her. His wife Kimberly smiled the whole time. Daisy needed a ride to the line shack but she walked almost the whole way until Ray, a cowboy she'd known since she was a young girl, found her and gave her a ride out to the shack. It concerned him, and he didn't want her staying in it. But he gave her his six-shooter and bullets before he left.

She'd told Ray what happened with her mail order groom, omitting the fact that she had shot the scoundrel. Then she told him she just wanted to be alone. At least once a week she found food supplies on the steps leading to the shack. He was a generous soul. And she often wondered why he lived his life without a wife.

He'd known her father and had been on the ranch since forever, so she never felt she had to hide from him, yet he left the supplies when she was sleeping.

Dale never even made sure she was still alive. He hadn't given her one thing. Everything she owned she'd gotten herself. There was a beautiful wardrobe she moved a couple yards every time she went scrounging. It was too heavy but bit by bit she'd get it here. She was glad for the six-shooter but wished for a rifle. There were plenty of wolves around. She'd built a bar lock to keep them out and had to reinforce the wooden shutters on her one window.

Chinking was next on her list. She'd fill the cracks between the pieces of wood with mud mixed with grass. It would keep the wind out and if the wolves couldn't look in and see her they might not think of her as easy prey. It would make it warmer too and maybe she wouldn't have to burn so much wood come winter.

She'd found a saw but no axe. It was better than nothing but it was a lot of work. Her hands had been a mass of bleeding blisters until the hard callouses formed. Solitude was nice, but at night she wished Sterling had loved her. Her heart hurt still, but the hurt would go away—at least that's what she told herself.

He was probably almost all healed and would be working. Would he work with the horses too? Or was he more of a cattle man? He never mentioned a sweetheart but maybe he didn't want his girl to see him wounded.

She'd had so much time to ask him questions and now she regretted that she hadn't. His gray eyes drew her in first. When they had first met, there had been no expression in them that showed he was uncomfortable about the way she looked. He'd smiled at her plenty, and he seemed to come to trust her.

Sondra had been right about how it looked, though. A single man and a single woman didn't live together. Why hadn't Georgie mentioned the gossip to her? Perhaps Sterling had been right; she was nursing him so it was very different. Despite her mother teaching her proper etiquette she didn't know all the ways of the social world and how it all worked.

There was a new doctor in town, and that relieved her. But if another sickness broke out, she'd stay away from it.

Grabbing her bucket, she went down to the stream. She kneeled down and caught her reflection in the water. It had been a while since she'd seen herself. It was almost worse than she remembered. Tears filled her eyes, and she quickly wiped them away. She didn't have time for pity. She had enough to do to get ready to survive the winter.

THERE WAS ONLY a month or so before winter. The nights had gotten so freezing and the stove in the line cabin didn't seem to do much to heat the small area. At least she had a hat and gloves that she'd crocheted. She was almost finished with a shawl. It was all kinds of colors, but she was blessed to have found the yarn. Her wardrobe now sat on the side of the shack. It was weather worn yet beautiful. Right now, it helped block the wind. More chinking would have to be added.

Her garden had yielded many vegetables. It had been a bountiful harvest, more than she could use. This morning she'd found canning jars on her steps. Ray was an angel. He seemed to know what she needed. She'd get busy canning the tomatoes and green beans first. She didn't have much storage space, but she'd build a wall of jars against another wall.

In all of her foraging trips she'd found nothing to use to build on to the house. A log house was her only option and they'd have to be small logs. She'd have plenty of time to figure it out during the winter months. Yes, she'd can this morning and saw some wood this afternoon. Then she'd check her snares for rabbits. She could can the meat too.

Many of her burdens had been lifted, and she thanked God. Sometimes she wished she'd never gone to Sweet Water. Fletcher's rejection only validated Dale and Kimberly's opinions. She wouldn't have fallen for a wounded man. She had foolishly thought herself to be immune to that emotion since she'd felt nothing for any man besides contempt before. Now there were times she felt hollow inside.

He'd held her hand that last night. It had made her heart soar and she was so glad to be there with him. He never said a word about even liking her. He never kissed her. There seemed to be many nevers, but what little that had happened she'd relive forever.

She had to put him from her mind, though, before she turned crazy. He was the past, not the present, and certainly not the future. Canning just a small portion of her harvest took all morning. She rested for about a quarter of an hour and then got her saw out. The wood could only be so long or it wouldn't fit in the cook stove.

She wished she could ask Ray to have a cup of coffee with her, but he'd always been a loner.

She wiped the sweat from her forehead with a cloth she kept in her apron pocket and looked along the horizon. She must be seeing things. A rider was coming her way. She pulled her gun out of the holster that she now wore and waited. It wasn't Ray and it wasn't Dale. She might as well get a drink of water. It would take a while for the rider to get to her place.

She dipped her cup into the bucket of cool water and sat on the steps with her gun in her lap. She was more curious than scared. Maybe she could get the drop on him and make him sit and talk with her for a while. She almost smiled at her musings.

She needed a cat. She wanted a dog but there wasn't room for one. The rider got closer, and still she didn't recognize him. Now she was nervous. What did he want? He looked to be bigger than the average man. His hat was brown and worn. He wasn't new to ranching or farming, from what she could tell. His horse was a fine quarter horse. A paint with lovely markings.

He stopped a ways away. "Miss Weathers? Are you Miss Weathers? Doctor Benz sent me. He said you should come."

"Something happen to my brother?"

"Not that I know of ma'am." He took his hat off. "We had a new group of travelers come through town three days ago and they brought the smallpox. Now we've been told you survived. Doctor Benz asked me to bring you back to town."

She rubbed her forehead while she shook her head.

Surely she had heard him wrong. She stared at him and was surprised he stared back.

"You're new in town, aren't you?" she asked.

"Yes. I'm Liam McCoy. I bought the old Reynolds place. My wife and children are sick. People in town didn't think I should bother you and they have barred me from tending to them."

"Got them all in the schoolhouse?"

"Yes, ma'am. I'm at my wits end. No one is there to help except the doctor. I was told not to hope because they're gonna die." His voice cracked.

"It's a possibility. I don't think they'd let me in. I tended their families and nearly died myself. They blamed me for the ones that died. That's why I'm living out here. No one else will have me around. They make fun of the way I look. I gave each tender care right up to the end. I prayed with them and for them." She shook her head. "I just can't"

"Please, Mrs. Wilson said children always die. She tried to discourage me from coming out here. Your brother tried to warn me off too. I can see the compassion in your eyes. Come with me."

How could she say no? It would lead to a bad end, but she had to try. "No one will help?"

"No, and the doc looks plumb worn out."

"I'll have to ride double with you."

"Fine. Could we go now?"

"Let me change real quick. I'll be back out before you know it." She went into the house and grabbed a pair of trousers she wore when she went far from the house. What did it matter what people thought? She threw a few things in a bag.

She closed the door as she left and put her foot in the stirrups and swung up behind him. She'd made the right choice with the trousers. "I can't promise they'll live."

"As long as they are being looked after."

She didn't answer she just hung on to his waist as they rode.

Her heart pounded as they hit the outskirts of the town. She didn't hold any respect for these people. She stared at Mr. McCoy's back the rest of the ride. She pretended she didn't hear people shouting for her to leave. When he stopped in front of the schoolhouse, she jumped down.

Mrs. Wilson pushed her way to the front. "Get! We don't want you here."

"I'm only here to look after the McCoy family." She turned and went to the door. She heard some rumbling about her only looking after one family. People were never happy.

Dr. Benz looked as though he hadn't slept in days. No one else was inside to help. There were other survivors in town. Why hadn't they volunteered to help? "I'm Daisy."

"Just call me Benz or Doc." He looked her up and down. "You are a Godsend. I can't keep up with everything that needs to be done."

"I'll try cooling a few off with water. Do you have ginger or garlic tea for the fever?"

"I have water."

Her jaw dropped. "Surely you have willow bark tea for the pain?"

"I can't get close enough to anyone in this town to tell them what I need."

Daisy went to the front door and opened it. She stepped outside. "We need clean sheets, clean cloths, cool water—lots and lots of water. Ginger or garlic to break the fever and willow bark for the pain."

People glanced away.

"Oh no you don't!" she snapped. "I'll come out among you and get what I need. I refuse to allow people to suffer like you did last time. So what will it be? Will you gather supplies or shall I?" She took a few steps in their direction.

Mr. McCoy stepped forward. "I'll get as much as I can. What do you need first?"

"We need to get the fever down so water, clothes first then we'll make a tea from the ginger and garlic the stronger the better. I will also throw soiled items out the back door. They must be burned. Ask around. There are others here that can't catch smallpox again. They should have stepped up. Thank you, Mr. McCoy. I will be sure to give your family extra care."

She walked back in and closed the door. There were plenty of gasps.

"Thank you," Benz said.

"It can be overwhelming, but if we take one step at a time, we can get to all the patients. We'll be getting plenty more people. Some people can go over a week before showing any signs." She grabbed cloths and a bucket. "Take a rest."

He nodded gratefully.

"Which of you is Mrs. McCoy?" asked Daisy.

By midafternoon, she had made the rounds at least once. Everyone had their heads bathed in cool water. She did what she could to make them comfortable. There were too many on the floor. It must be beyond uncomfortable.

The crowd outside threw something against the front door, probably a rock. She opened it and was astonished by the amount of supplies she saw. She looked for and smiled at Mr. McCoy. "Your wife is lovely. So far they seem to have light cases." Then she panned the crowd. "Go home. You'll only spread it to one another. You don't know for days you have it and by then, everyone you came in contact with has caught smallpox. I know you're all worried, but I'll come out when I can and give you updates."

"Where's the doctor?" one man shouted.

Mrs. Wilson pushed to the front. "You wouldn't know the truth if it bit you. I only want to hear from the doctor."

"You wore him out by not helping him. Just hope you don't end up in here, Mrs. Wilson. I treat people with the same kindness they have shown me over the last years. Good day." She felt guilty about what she'd said to Mrs. Wilson but that woman had been the first to call her unsightly and not fit to be out in the daylight.

She went back out and brought in the supplies, heartened to see that food for her and the doctor had been included. She crushed garlic and chopped ginger and put it on to boil. Then she helped to change sheets for those who couldn't do for themselves. It gladdened her heart to see them helping each other.

Many had the rash. So the illness couldn't have been from the people who traveled through a few days ago. It took much longer for the rash to appear than that. Daisy sighed, already tired. She'd be here for a while. After finding another pot, she started on the willow bark tea. Wouldn't Glory, Letty, and Georgie be proud of her? Oh, how she missed them.

"How long did I sleep?" Benz glanced around and scrunched his forehead. "How?"

Daisy offered him a smile. "They brought the supplies, and I got busy. Everyone here is in dire need, but I found if you start at one side of the room and work toward the other side it's easier than running around. I sure wish there was a cure for smallpox."

Benz smiled a sad smile. "I wish there was too. Is that garlic and ginger boiling?"

"Yes and willow bark. I'll start off with the garlic and ginger mix then if they keep that down I'll give them tea made from the willow bark. That is, if it's all right with you? There might be new ways since I had the pox."

"No, you're doing just fine. Some doctors still believe in bloodletting." He shuddered; apparently he did not subscribe to that belief. "I thought the folks in this town were decent folks. Now I'm not so sure. Not one volunteered to help, and I know others here are immune."

"They're afraid they'll get blamed for all the deaths like I was. I almost never come to town anymore."

"Why are you living in a line shack?" He turned his head and caught her in his gaze. "You'll freeze the first bad snow we have."

"I've been shoring it up, and it's warmer than it looks. I'll be just fine." She ladled the garlic ginger mix into a coffee pot.

"That doesn't answer the why. Your brother's house is large enough." He studied her, one eyebrow raised in query, and she glanced away.

"His wife wouldn't be able to eat if I was at the table," she mumbled. "They decided the line shack would be fine for me. I best get started." She walked away carrying the pot and several tin cups. The doc was right; she should have been given a place within the house. She *expected* to be mistreated.

"Mrs. McCoy, let's see if you can keep some of this down. It won't taste the best, but if you drink it your children might too. It's for fever. I'll be back after everyone gets this with tea to help with the pain. Your husband is a good man. He made sure we got the supplies we needed."

"We've been together since we were sixteen. He is the best man I know. We were getting settled when this happened." Her voice became hoarse. "He bought a ranch and cattle. An army friend has the cattle."

"That's an extra reason to fight to get better." Daisy took the cup and tended to the little McCoys. Children seemed to be the first to die. "I'm Daisy. I need you to drink this." She looked into the blue eyes of a small child with strawberry blond hair. The girl drank it down without complaint. The little boy refused, and she spooned whatever she could into his mouth. He wanted his mother.

Daisy rearranged their pallets, so he was on one side of his mother and the girl was on the other. It would make it harder to tend the mother but she'd make it work.

Most could drink down the first cup and later she gave them all willow bark tea. As she glanced around the room, her heart grew heavy. How many would survive?

CHAPTER ELEVEN

*T*wo weeks later, Daisy walked out the front door and sat down. So many were dying, and this morning both Mrs. McCoy and her son were dead. It had gotten to be too much, and she finally broke down in tears. She just wanted a moment alone, but people were outside waiting for word on their kin.

Someone shouted at her. She looked up and saw Mr. McCoy. It would break her heart to tell him. She got up and walked to some predetermined unmarked line in the grass. "Mr. McCoy, your wife and son died this morning. I'm so sorry. They weren't in any pain thanks to you. Your daughter's rash looks to be going away. I'll look after her." She couldn't stand the grief in his eyes but she managed to hold his gaze rather than looking away.

"Sure you will, just like you've looked after all the ones that died!" someone yelled.

She kept walking until something hit her in the back. Sharp pain radiated outward, bringing tears to her eyes. She turned and spotted a hand-sized rock on the ground. She closed her eyes and steeled herself against the hatred as she went back into the school. Her back hurt something awful but there was work to do.

They had one other person helping, but he was making a lot of money doing it, the undertaker. He hired two men to come and take away the dead. He didn't get near the bodies until they nailed the coffins shut.

She wanted to resent his monetary gain but who else would take the dead?

"Daisy you're back is bleeding through your shirt."

She shrugged. "I'll be just fine."

"Let me look at it." Benz said in his no nonsense voice.

He led her into the storage room where they'd been taking turns sleeping. She turned away, unbuttoned her shirt, making sure that her back was all he could see. When he touched her and put a salve and a bandage on it, she felt nothing. That made her miss Sterling even more. It wasn't just that he was a man; it was because of his compassion and his gentleness. No, that wasn't right the doc had those qualities too. Sterling just made her feel things, and she didn't need to know exactly why.

"What happened?" asked the doc, his voice carrying shock.

"Someone from the crowd threw a rock at me. They're blaming the deaths on me once again."

He turned her around and looked into her eyes. "They blame you? But why?"

"I survived last time and the doctor died, and no one would come to help even though their family members were in here. I had watched the doctor for days and knew what to do but people died, anyway."

"Of course they did. There is no cure for smallpox. I can't help but notice that there are only white people in here."

"The freedmen are not allowed in most places in this town. They have their own doctor. They're also not as foolish. They all stay clear of each other until the sickness is over, and they help each other."

"How do they stay clear of each other?"

"All the people with sick family members stay in their home and others do for them. Bring food, supplies, anything needed. They stop the spread of the pox."

"Very smart," the doc said, bobbing his head in approval. "I'll go out there and announce the deaths from now on. I hope they don't take to stoning me too." He gestured toward her back. "I'll check your wound again later."

She nodded and went back to work. Exhaustion filled every limb, but she needed to keep going. Her heart hurt. Couldn't people see she was doing the right thing? Whatever happened to helping others? She didn't understand. Where was Reverend Ludwig? Or had he been replaced? Reverend Ludwig had never lifted a finger to help her. She had even gone to him with her troubled heart, and he didn't give her words of comfort. Not even quote from the Bible.

She had found her own solace in God's Word.

Ephesians 4:32 — *And be ye kind one to another, tenderhearted, forgiving one another, even as God for Christ's sake hath forgiven you.*

She ladled willow bark tea into the coffee pot and thought of the hate-filled townspeople. Had none of them read their Bibles? What about what Peter had said?

Finally, [be ye] all of one mind, having compassion one of another, love as brethren, [be] pitiful, [be] courteous: Not rendering evil for evil, or railing for railing: but contrariwise blessing; knowing that ye are thereunto called, that ye should inherit a blessing. or he that will love life, and see good days, let him refrain his tongue from evil, and his lips that they speak no guile: Let him eschew evil, and do good; let him seek peace, and ensue it. For the eyes of the Lord [are] over the righteous, and his ears [are open]

123

unto their prayers: but the face of the Lord [is] against them that do evil.

Was she mistaking the meaning of the words? That couldn't be. God was love, God was goodness. No, she wasn't the mistaken one.

After she made sure that all who could still swallow had their tea, she wiped each brow and face with clean water. When that was done she took little Ellie McCoy in her lap. The child was sick, confused, and scared. The poor girl was maybe two at the most. As she rocked her, Daisy prayed that Ellie would be spared.

FOUR MONTHS and not a word from Daisy. Sterling was sure she hadn't gotten even one of his telegrams or letters. She would have acknowledged him and told him to leave her be if that was what she wanted.

He rode his bay gelding into town and right off noticed a gathering. Anger and sadness was written on all the people's faces. He hated to interrupt, but he needed directions to the Weathers' ranch. He rode closer to the group and got off his horse. After tying the reins to the hitching post, he walked over to the crowd.

"What happened?" he asked one woman.

She turned and looked him up and down before she nodded at him. "Smallpox."

"Have there been many deaths?" he asked. It was a devastating illness.

"Too many, if you ask me. The doctor insisted that the Weathers girl be brought to help. She caused so many deaths last time. She just came to tell this poor man his wife and child were dead."

Sterling turned. "I'm sorry for your loss."

"Thank you." The grief-stricken man shook his head as his gaze darted around the gathered crowd. "I don't understand why they think Daisy causes the deaths. She looked completely worn out when she came out to tell me. Then some yahoo threw a big rock and it hit her. My daughter is still in there, and I have faith that the doc and Daisy are doing the best they can."

"Daisy is for sure. She has the biggest heart of anyone I've ever met."

The woman stared at him in disdain. "You, sir, are an outsider to these parts. We know what happened before and what's going on now."

"Then why aren't you in there making sure they are getting the care they need?" Disgust filled him. This was the kind of treatment that had hurt Daisy before, had made her feel unworthy of love. "I'm surprised Daisy offered to help again after you blamed her and insulted her. People in this town told her she was too ugly to be in their town. She's had enough rejection and hurt for two lifetimes."

The woman heaved her shoulders and lifted her chin. "I am Mrs. Wilson. I'm the matriarch of this fine town. Watch what you say."

Sterling gave her a quick nod and walked back toward his horse. He talked to a few people and found that Daisy had been in there almost a month and no new cases had been reported for two weeks now. He got instructions to the Weathers' farm. He wanted to meet Dale and his wife before he sought out Daisy. His anger grew as he rode along the road.

Her heart was too tender, and she was too kind. Only one man had spoken up for Daisy. What kind of people were they?

The farm looked well kept. It surprised him to see two houses. He rode up to the white fence in front of the house and got off his horse. He'd expected some pain after the long ride but he was fine. He had the slightest limp, and it didn't bother him one bit.

The front door opened before he even opened the fence gate. A big man with brown hair and eyes wearing a sullen look came outside. "State your business and leave."

Sterling cocked his brow. "I'm here to inquire about your sister. How is she?"

"She ain't here. Besides, I decided you're not suitable for her."

"You know nothing about me."

"I know enough. My sister is my business. She ain't marrying a cripple," Dale yelled.

"Well that's in my favor then. She might consider me."

"You've been bedridden. Daisy slaved to take care of you, and you sent her home. There is no place for her."

"How far out is the line shack?" Sterling asked angrily.

"Dale, what's going on?" A petite blond stepped out from the house.

"He's looking for Daisy."

This must be Dale's wife, the one who didn't want Daisy around. She took her time looking Sterling over. "You must have Daisy mixed up with someone else. Daisy had an illness, and now it's unbearable to look upon her face. Would you like to come inside?"

"The house looks big and there is another house over there. Who lives there?"

"Our foreman," she said.

"How big is his family?"

"Whose family?" she tilted her head.

"The foreman. He must have a family to warrant a house of his own."

"No, Stan lives there alone."

"Enough with the questions, like I said Sterling, you're

not suitable for my sister." Dale turned and pushed his wife into the house.

"What happened to my letters?"

Dale turned and smiled. "I used them to start fires."

Sterling leveled his most intense glare at Dale while hovering his hand over his gun. "Where is the line shack?"

"Due west, but she's not there," he said smugly

"I know."

Sterling swung up and turned his horse. Then he rode west. What a nitwit. He did not have one care for his sister and neither did his wife. He shuddered. All she had was wandering eyes.

The shack rose in front of him, and Sterling was relieved there weren't any animals that needed tending. He expected if there had been any, they would dead by now. He left his horse to graze while he went into the shack. A smile spread across his face. She'd filled in the gaps with chinking. Filled jars were stacked up against one wall. There were odds and ends like the chair out front. Her wood pile was pitiful, though.

There was always the chance she'd send him away, and before he left, he wanted to be sure she'd survive the winter. Looking around, he didn't find an axe. He did see a saw. That explained why the logs of wood were skinny. She needed an axe and he needed to find a place to stay.

Back to town he went. He located a boarding house close to the school in order to see her when she came outside. He ate with the rest of the boarders but didn't bring her name up. He didn't want to feel tempted to hit anyone.

There wasn't much going on at night. He made it to the general store before they closed and bought a book and an axe. It was getting dark. He saw someone creep around the school and then sit down. As soon as the person bent her head, he knew it was Daisy.

He slowly made his way toward her. He didn't want to frighten her.

"I've got my gun trained on you, mister. Put the axe down."

He suppressed a grin. "Still have your spunk, I see."

She jumped up. "Sterling?"

"It's me. I came to see why you never answered any of my letters."

She shook her head. "What letters? There were letters?"

He heard the tears in her voice. "There were. Your brother took them."

She sighed loudly. "I'm not surprised." She leaned forward and squinted. "My eyes are adjusting to the darkness. You look healthy."

"I had a great nurse." He grinned.

"Oh? I'm glad you did. Is she staying at the ranch?" She didn't sound so glad.

"She left and I'm hoping to get her back. I can't come any closer can I?"

"No, but I have a little girl who is ready to go home. Her mother and brother died. Her father will be here tomorrow, though. He comes every day. He's the only one who brings supplies. I don't understand what is wrong with the people in this town. It's been exhausting, so many died, and I hear they are blaming me again. Why? Why Sterling? How could it possibly be my fault?"

"I wish I could take you into my arms, sweetheart. As soon as this is over you're coming with me." He held his breath.

"Where would you take me? There is only one place where I'm alone and no one can say awful things about me. I have my line shack." She sounded so resigned.

He'd wait until she was away from all the death to talk about her coming home with him. She might be more receptive after he kissed her. "I saw where you live. You've done well getting ready for winter. I bought the axe to chop some wood for you."

"You don't have to do that."

"Call it repayment for all you did for me."

She hesitated and then nodded. "Thank you. I need to go back in. I hope to see you again."

"Goodnight, sweetheart." He turned and walked away. Maybe she wasn't interested in a relationship with him. Maybe he'd gotten it all wrong.

He sure hoped not.

EARLY NEXT MORNING, Daisy looked out the window for Mr. McCoy. She cleaned Ellie as well as she could. Took her old dress off and wrapped her in a clean sheet. "Wait by the door. I'll look for your father."

The girl stared with eyes that looked too big on her gaunt face.

Daisy stepped outside and spotted Mr. McCoy instantly. She smiled at him and nodded. "Remember, a nice warm bath as soon as she gets home."

He simply nodded.

She opened the door and Ellie ran, though slow because she was weak, to her father. He scooped her up and closed his eyes. He opened them, and they shimmered as he yelled, "Thank you, Daisy."

Tears ran down her face as she watched him carry Ellie away. No one ever said thank you in this town. She was so tempted to run from the school and never come back. What would it matter? The doctor saved the ones who lived, and the ones that died were deemed her fault. It would be wonderful if she were the one Sterling was looking for. It hurt, and she wished she could be happy for him, but it just wouldn't come. She didn't see him in the crowd, so he must be chopping wood.

At least she'd be warm this winter. God was looking out for her. She'd have her Bible, and she'd read it, trying to understand why some called themselves righteous while being cruel. She'd have the last laugh when they encountered her in heaven if they got in.

She turned to go into the school and was pelted by several rocks this time. One hit her head and she almost went down. She got inside as quickly as she could before she fell to her knees. She reached for a cloth and held it against the back of her head.

"I'll go outside from now on," Benz said. "It's dangerous for you. I've come to the conclusion this isn't the town for me." He examined her head and wound gauze around her forehead to keep the bandage in place.

"I feel like the walking wounded."

"You look like it."

"WHAT DO you mean someone hit her in the head with a rock? She could be hurt!" Sterling roared to the young man who told him. Looking around no one else seemed to think it was wrong. "Where is the preacher? He should be here praying with all of you."

"He stays indoors where it is safe," Mrs. Wilson told him in a haughty voice.

"What about the dying? Don't they need spiritual comfort?"

"If we could burn the witch in there, none of this would be happening."

Too many people looked eager to start the fire. Enough

was enough. These people didn't deserve her help. He strode forward and opened the school door. He went in and grabbed Daisy up in his arms. "Sorry, Doc, they're planning to burn her to the stake. She's coming with me." He didn't wait for any reply. He held her tight in one arm, but his gun was drawn and clutched in his free hand.

He would have thought at least one person would have said something about the bandage wrapped around her head. He shook his head in disgust. They looked so smug in their belief that they were better than her. He sat her astride the horse then mounted and wrapped her in his arms. They rode off with her practically sitting in his lap. He pulled her toward him so she could have something to lean against.

His heart hurt for her. The circles under her eyes were from weeks of less than adequate sleep. She'd lost weight and looked as though a good wind could carry her away. His poor love. He should have insisted she come away with him the moment he'd arrived, but he also knew she had an independent streak.

"Where are you taking me?" she whispered.

"First to the line shack and then home."

"No. My brother won't allow me to live in the house."

"If I have my way, you'll never see him again. He's a sorry excuse for a man. There is never a reason to be so cruel. You are enough. In my eyes, you are more than enough, and I'm sure that God must feel the same way. You have given of yourself when the town preacher couldn't be bothered to pray with the sick. There is evil in that town. We'll grab what you need and head out. I don't want a mob hoping to burn you coming our way."

She was so still it scared him. Once at the shack he gently lifted her down. Taking her hand, he led her into the dwelling. There wasn't room for the both of them.

"Can you pack a bag or two? I'm taking you with me. I

have supplies so just pack what you need." She looked so very lost, and he wasn't sure the sadness in her eyes would ever go away. He'd do everything within his power to show her that she was worthy of love.

She stepped out with a bulging carpet bag. He took it from her and tied it to the back of the horse behind the saddle. He lifted her, but she didn't look at him. He grew more and more worried as they rode on. She never said a word.

"Everyone at the ranch will be happy to see you. Lydia and Gabriel live in the house we were in. I'm staying at the bunkhouse, and Georgie asked me to tell you to come home and you're welcome to stay with her."

She acted as though she didn't hear him. Discouraged, he didn't know what else to say. They rode for most of the day, and he found a shady spot near a stream for them to set up camp. Once they unloaded the horse, she looked at the supplies and started making something.

"The stream looks inviting," he said.

She looked in the stream's direction and shrugged her shoulders before going back to work. Her work seemed to take all her concentration. He watched her, hoping to come up with a way to get through to her.

She served bacon and beans. She ate little, and she looked worn to the bone. He filled a pot with water, and after they finished eating, he took a towel and soap out of his saddlebags.

"It's too cold to wash in the stream, but I heated some water, and I have a towel and soap. You can wash up while I wash the dishes at the stream."

Her eyes flickered, and she nodded. He waited a long while before he returned. She sat in front of the fire with a clean dress on, and she was brushing her wet hair. Her skin looked red as though she'd scrubbed herself too hard.

"Where did you get the soap? It smells wonderful."

He grinned. "Different, isn't it? Glory makes soap now and then I've been told. This one is lavender and rosemary. At first I thought it a joke, but it smells like either a man or woman could use it."

"This is the best I've felt in months. Thank you, Sterling." She swallowed hard and drew a deep breath. "I can't wait to meet the woman who nursed you. The one you talked about bringing home." Her slight smile turned into a grim frown.

"We've all missed you," he said as a wave of sadness washed over him. "I thought I'd never see you again. I remembered the line shack and promised myself to get you out of there as soon as I could. I worked extra hard to strengthen my leg. You don't deserve to be locked away. I wish there was a way to make you believe in yourself. I believe it'll take time. Words don't just disappear. Sometimes they burrow inside of you, and it's hard to get rid of them."

"You sound as though it happened to you too. You explained it so well."

"They called me a cripple a couple times while I was in town, in Spring Water. We all went to watch the Union Soldiers leave."

"Is that a good thing? Will law and order still exist there?"

He nodded. "Parker and Max are taking turns being sheriff until they find one they can hire. We know the KKK will be back, but since we know who is in it, we can tell when they are going for a ride. Parker put them in jail but the judge let them out. Parker plans to have men there every time they try to harm anyone."

"When do his men ever get any sleep?"

Sterling laughed. "He hired on several men. We built another bunk house."

"That's good. I will save my money and make a life for myself. I heard that sometimes a widower needs someone to take care of the children fairly quickly after his wife dies. That might happen to me."

"I'm sure the man who is lucky enough to get you will be proud to have you as his wife."

"I'm tired." She stood and got her bedroll. After spreading it out by the fire, she lay down and was almost instantly asleep.

He put an extra blanket on her. She looked exhausted even in her sleep. He wanted to tell her of his feelings, but she was too emotionally fragile. She'd be sure to tell him no. They had a friendship, and he'd build upon it. He wished he was more experienced in such matters.

Thank you, Lord for keeping her safe. Thank you for hearing my pleas and for always being there. I never ride alone; I know You are with me.

He spread out his bedroll on the opposite side of the fire and was soon asleep.

CHAPTER TWELVE

They were almost at the ranch and butterflies filled her stomach. Did they want her back? Sterling never said staying with Georgie included a job. What would they think now she'd spent a few nights alone with Sterling? He was always the perfect gentleman.

She was still so weary. She wanted to sleep in the comfortable bed in Georgie's extra room. She wanted to feel like she belonged. Once again, she wished she had her extra-large bonnet. She'd need to make a new one.

They rode past a few guards who nodded to them. Then she saw the houses come into view. It felt like a homecoming, but she warned herself not to get attached to the place. It would only lead to misery.

Parker and Georgie hurried outside, and Parker lifted her down. "We're glad you came back, Daisy. It was like a part of the family was missing."

Georgie hurried and hugged her extra tight. It was the nicest homecoming Daisy'd ever had.

Sterling swung out of the saddle, and Kent grabbed his horse and led it to the barn. Sterling wasn't ready to let Daisy go just yet. He followed the rest into the house. He was taken aback to see Sondra taking care of the young ones. He ignored her and sat down next to Daisy on the settee.

He took Daisy's trembling hand in his and gave it a small squeeze.

"Daisy, are you unwell?" Georgie asked.

"No. There was smallpox near my family's farm. I helped."

"I'm so glad the community is embracing you."

Sterling shook his head. "I got her out of there while they were discussing burning her at the stake. I've never met people like I met there, and I never want to see any of them again. Georgie was living at the schoolhouse, tending the sick for almost over a month. Talk about ungrateful!"

"I wish I knew what to say to offer you comfort, Daisy. We're glad you're back, and I want you to consider this ranch your home."

Daisy smiled. "I think I'll take you up on that. I have had little rest the last few weeks."

"Sterling, why don't you carry in Daisy's things and put them into the room. Sleep well, Daisy, I'll wake you for supper."

"Thank you." Daisy went into the familiar room and breathed in deep. It'd been a long time since she'd felt so welcomed. She smiled at Sterling as he carried her bag into the room. He put it on her bed and stared at her for a moment. He opened his arms and she couldn't get there fast enough.

The sound of his heart under her ear filled her with joy, and she would hold on to that feeling as long as she could. Soon she'd meet the woman who had caught his eye and heart. It would take everything inside her to wish them well.

"You should let others know you're back. I'm sure you were missed." She stepped back and looked into his eyes. "Does she live on the ranch or is she from town?"

He tilted his head as though he had to think about it. "She lives here. I'll let you sleep." He closed the door behind him.

What was all the mystery? He acted as though he didn't want to talk about the woman who'd nursed him. Maybe he was just being sensitive. What did she know about men, anyway? She removed her dress and slipped under the covers. The bed felt so big compared to the little strip of mattress she'd had in the shack.

———

STERLING WASHED UP FOR SUPPER. He'd been invited to eat at the house, and he was eager to see Daisy again. But what if she said no? What if she didn't want him? What if she said yes out of obligation or something? Was it too soon? She did need to build up her strength. Maybe he should wait until the time was right, but he couldn't keep answering her questions about the "other" woman who'd supposedly nursed him. He had never meant to deceive her, but she'd never guessed he was talking about her.

She was safe and on the ranch, and that is all that mattered. Winter would come, and then he'd have to wait until spring for a house to be built. In the meantime, how could he make certain she didn't leave again?

He needed a real plan, and he needed one quick.

He walked into the Eastman house and was able to watch Daisy for a moment without her knowing. Her dress was a faded calico and she was thin, but he thought her beautiful. She'd think he was teasing if he told her, though.

She turned and smiled at him, and his heart beat a little faster as he returned her smile.

"You look fetching," he said.

Her eyes opened as though she didn't believe him. "We

have most of the food on the table. You're welcome to come sit."

He nodded and took off his hat then placed it on a table next to the door. He'd missed her something awful and here she was.

"Good evening, Georgie."

"Nice to see you, Sterling. Please take a seat."

He sat down. Where was Parker? He didn't see any of the children about either.

"I have to hurry over to Mary Beth's house. I'm dining there. I hope you two don't mind eating alone." A spark flickered in her eyes.

"Don't let us keep you. I could walk you over if you like."

"Sterling, you are always a gentleman, but Parker is watching for me." She kissed Daisy on the cheek before she hurried out the door.

Daisy stood there looking surprised. "She didn't say a thing the whole time she made supper. She wouldn't allow me to help her. I wonder what's going on."

Sterling stood and rounded the table until they were toe to toe. He reached down and took her hands in his. "You don't have a clue, do you?"

"No. Georgie didn't say a word. It's odd, don't you think?"

"Not odd, more like meddling... but good meddling."

"I don't understand. Sterling, what is going on?"

He swooped down and settled his lips on hers. She stepped back and put her hand over her mouth while she stared at him. He could see the question in her eyes.

"I care for you, Daisy." He tried to sound confident.

"What about the woman who nursed you? What would she have to say?" she asked in a slightly bitter voice.

"Oh Daisy, haven't you figured it out? You are that woman. You are the woman I care for. When you left, I almost went crazy. There was no way I could follow in my condition. First I was mad, then I was hurt, then I became determined to win you back. But I can't even try if you think there is another woman involved."

"I don't understand."

"I know you don't." He gentled his tone. "You don't give yourself enough credit. You are enough just the way you are. I see you as a beautiful woman who would give her heart and soul to the right man. A woman who never thinks of herself first, a woman who can be a partner in a marriage, a good marriage. A woman who was meant to enjoy life, have a home and a family. You deserve to have a man who loves all of you. When I look at you, I don't see imperfection; you are fairer than any. I see a woman full of goodness and love. I see the woman I love."

She took another step back and shook her head as her eyes filled with tears. "You just feel sorry for me. Don't mistake your feelings for anything else. I already know no man would ever want me, and I've come to terms with that. Does it make me cry at night? Sometimes. But then I count my many blessings. You'll be sorry the first morning you have to eat breakfast across from me. You'll see every imperfection there is." Her chin wobbled as she shook her head again. "Don't throw your life away."

"Is that how you feel? You don't have any feeling for me?"

"What I want doesn't matter. I learned that lesson years ago. You're the best friend I've ever had and I wouldn't be able to bear it if you turned away from me because you could no longer stand the sight of me. What you really feel is pity. You're sorry for me. You're outraged at how I was treated, and I understand the urge to defend a friend. That's all it is." She stared into his eyes with sad tears in hers. "I'm sorry. I'm so tired. Sterling, you'll be thanking me."

He watched her walk back into her bedroom. What had just occurred? He poured out his heart, and she told him he was wrong. How did that end up happening? He shook his head and grabbed his hat. He walked out of the house and sat on the porch until the Eastman clan came home.

Parker sat next to him. "Didn't go as planned?"

"No. She's convinced she's saving me by saying no. She thinks one day I'll wake up and find myself unable to bear the way she looks. I don't have charming words to counter her concerns. She said it's my urge to protect a friend. I don't understand any of it. She cares for me. I can see it in her eyes. There is so much sorrow in her eyes too."

Parker stared up at the sky. "I'll just have to arrange it that you two work together. Maybe once she feels better—"

"I'd rather you didn't, Parker. I'll figure something out. I appreciate your offer, though." He stood and wandered down the steps and then into the bunkhouse.

He sat with the men, only half listening to their banter. Now what? He didn't have a clue.

"GOOD MORNING," Georgie greeted. "Did you sleep well?"

"I love the bed, but my mind wouldn't quiet. It's all so confusing. I can't understand Sterling. I know he means well, but I ended up feeling worse. I want a husband and children more than anything, but it's not going to happen for me. He tried to make me feel better last night by using sweet words. Does he think I haven't looked in a mirror or heard the awful taunts from people? He needs to stay away. I won't have his life ruined by him tying himself to me. I'll be fine by myself. It's better that way. He'll realize I'm right about this."

"What if he really loves you? Won't you be throwing away a chance at happiness? You're all he's talked about since you left. He grieved for you. I thought he'd have a setback, but he became determined to bring you back and marry you."

"I set him straight." She paused then said, "Did the offer for me to stay here also include a job?"

"Of course, Daisy."

Relief washed over her. She could stay. Would Sterling eventually take a wife and live in a house on the ranch? Likely he would. The thought pained her so much she wanted to double over. She'd been through emotional hurt before but that would be the worst. If she prepared herself, though, she just might make it through.

"I do want you to regain your strength first."

Daisy nodded, made short work of eating breakfast, and then cleaned the table. She would have washed the dishes, but Georgie shooed her out of the house.

Feeling at loose ends, she visited with Lydia. It wasn't a far walk by any means, but it tired her. Lydia was excited to see her and they sat on the porch.

"Everyone missed you! Especially Sterling, he ended up with a fever right after you left and he kept calling for you and wouldn't calm until Glory pretended to be you. He held on to her for hours. Kent wasn't so pleased, but he understood. Then when Sterling's fever broke and he found out you weren't there, he grew silent. It was eerie. I feared for him. He refused to get out of bed or stretch his leg. Then one day he decided he needed to be able to ride a horse and quickly. That man worked so hard I thought he'd drop. But he sure was proud the day he left to go get you. I bet he's so happy to have you home."

Daisy felt things fall into place. He hadn't been trying to make her feel better, he cared. She needed to talk to him before he changed his mind. She'd been nothing but a fool, but she really didn't think anyone would call her beautiful. She loved Sterling and she sent him away from her. Now what? How did a woman woo a man?

When she got back to Georgie, Daisy asked for advice.

Georgie thought a picnic would be nice and helped to put everything needed into a basket. Now for the unnerving part; asking Sterling to go with her.

She had no idea what she would say, but she kept walking to the barn, anyway. There were plenty of cow hands around but no Sterling and to her surprise no looks of disgust.

"He's over by the second corral," Parker told her without being asked.

Her face heated as she thanked him. She stood in the shade and watched Sterling work with a big bay gelding. The bay was not cooperating, but Sterling looked just as determined. At long last, the horse gave in and went to Sterling, who praised the animal. He looked up and smiled when he saw her. He worked with the horse for a few minutes longer before handing it off to one of the horsemen. He bent and brushed the dust off his pants.

"I'm surprised to see you here. Last I heard you were supposed to be resting."

"I'm planning to. I have a picnic all ready to go but no escort, and I was hoping you'd come with me."

He stiffened for a moment and looked at her. "Sounds like a fine idea. I'll hitch up the buggy, and we can be on our way."

The quivering in her stomach wouldn't stop. How was she supposed to eat if her stomach wouldn't cooperate? What was she supposed to talk to Sterling about? She waiting in front of the barn and Sterling came out driving a very nice buggy.

He got down and helped her into it. "I have to say this is a surprise."

They started off.

Sudden apprehension overcame Daisy, and she pulled in a couple of deep breaths before she felt like she could speak. "I hardly slept last night. I tried to think of every motive you'd have to marry me, but I couldn't find one. Then I remembered we were best of friends, and you wouldn't lie to me. I also heard about your fever and not letting go of Glory."

"So you believe me?"

"Yes about most things, except I think you may need some of those spectacles some people wear to see correctly."

He took her hand in his. "Everyone sees things differently. Some people like a wooden house while some like Spanish looking ones. We're all different."

They rode in silence for a while before Sterling pulled up the reins. He helped her down and left his hands to linger longer than necessary. His warm palms against her waist felt nice. He grabbed the basket while she carried the blanket. They walked toward a creek, and it surprised her to see a waterfall.

"It's beautiful!"

"I've come here to shower a few times. The cold water helped my leg."

"I bet it feels wonderful having the water wash over you." She unfolded the blanket and laid it on the ground. Then she sat in the middle and took the basket he handed her. He was silent as he sat and watched her take items out of the basket.

"You're a truthful man, a man of character and integrity. What I mean is you don't just say pretty words to a woman because she wants to hear them. You say them because you mean them. I've been giving this a lot of thought. I've known my feelings for a long while now and I don't want to lose you. I don't want to wake up someday and see you on the ranch with a wife and children. I'm tough, but not that tough. I thank you for telling me I'm beautiful and that you care for me." That took a lot of energy to get out.

"Daisy, I love you and I want you to be my wife. I want a family and a life with you. Will you marry me?"

"Yes, Sterling, I will marry you." She smiled as he gathered her in his arms and kissed her. She could feel his love in the powerful kiss. His strong arms would shelter her from any storm.

"Are you hungry?" She suddenly felt shy.

"Yes, I'm hungry."

They ate with pleasant conversation about trivialities, and after she packed the leftovers into the basket, she yawned.

"Lie down and take a rest. I'll guard you."

"I could just as easy take a nap back at the house."

He lay down and closed his eyes. She did the same, and when he offered her his hand, she took it. The sound of the waterfall soothed her.

Movement woke Daisy.

Sterling was over her, shaking her. "Wake up, we have company."

She sat up and patted her hair. "Who is that?"

Sterling sighed. "I believe it to be Sondra. Just follow my lead. Pretend to be fixing your dress."

She looked at him with questions in her eyes and went about smoothing out her dress.

Sondra drew closer. "I knew it! I knew you two would be out here sinning." The look on her face was smug.

"I haven't sinned. How about you, Daisy?"

"No, I didn't."

"We're a Christian community, and I'm afraid Daisy will have to leave since she cannot seem to contain herself."

"I guess there is only one thing to do." He got up on one knee. "Daisy, will you marry me?"

"Oh my! Of course I'll marry you." She glanced at Sondra. "Thank you. If not for you I doubt he'd have asked."

Sondra's jaw dropped. Then she snapped it shut and glared. "It doesn't erase you sins."

"What about bearing false witness or judging lest you be judged?" demanded Sterling. "I may not look like it, but I bet I know the Bible better than you do, though it doesn't make me more Christian than you. I'm tired of people making accusations in the name of our Lord when they have no idea what the whole story is. Have you asked forgiveness for the way you tried to shame us? How about for making Daisy leave? Was there goodness in your heart when you rode out here? There is nothing worse than someone thinking they are more righteous than another. Have you ever sympathized with anyone, or is your way the only way because you believe God is on your side?" He shook his head sadly. "I will keep you in my prayers, Sondra." Then he turned his back to her. How dare she try to ruin their engagement? What was wrong with her? Finally, he heard her ride away.

"Thank you, Sterling. I don't think anyone has ever defended me the way you just did."

"Does that make me your hero?" He took her hands and pulled her to a standing position. He cradled her face against his palms. "I do think you're beautiful. But Sondra isn't worth our time. I will pray for her like I said I would."

"Yes, you are my hero, always."

EPILOGUE

Winter was fighting to make an appearance, so they made the wedding small. Daisy took one last look in the mirror and nodded. Sterling had changed her own view of herself. He'd been right from the first when he called her scars badges of courage.

There was a light knock on the door, and then Georgie let herself in. She stared at Daisy with tears shimmering in her eyes.

"You are so lovely," she said after a moment. "You should know that Sondra and Walter didn't come, and I think that's a relief. I have to say out of all of us, I think your story is the most romantic."

Daisy's face grew warm. "Thank you, Georgie." She took one last look in the mirror. "I think it's time."

Georgie fixed Daisy's lace veil. "Your dress is so stunning. Sterling was so sweet to order you one from London."

"I suppose he wants me to feel like a princess, and he's doing a good job."

Georgie went out first and Daisy followed. The dress was

indeed beautiful. It was the dress she had admired in the dress store window her first day in Spring Water. It was a beautiful coral pink color and it was all trimmed in delicate lace. She felt fairer than any. She smiled at everyone as she walked to Sterling. Her life had been one of an outcast, and here she was getting married with her friends at her side.

God had made the impossible happen for her, and her heart was overflowing. They had built a new house in record time, and Sterling ordered the furniture. He'd inherited his family's great wealth. There had never been a reason for Bill to rob people. One day she and Sterling would ride out and she would show him where his brother was buried.

The smallest of barks were heard and she looked down at the tiny puppy Sterling had given her the day before. She'd told him about Rufus. She cried when he handed the puppy to her. She quickly declared that his name was Rufus.

One of the babies fussed, and that added to her happiness. She'd be able to have a family after all. Through the years, her faith had wavered, but she remained a firm believer. Daisy had talked to the preacher about being a Christian. He'd told her that no one was better than the other, no one should sit in judgement of others, for that was to be left to God.

It was time for Sterling to lift the veil, and her stomach clenched. For some reason she still sometimes thought he'd find her lacking. But he smiled at her now as though she was the most beautiful woman in the room. When the preacher told him he could kiss her, he dived right in and swept her off her feet as he kissed her. He finally came up for air when the preacher cleared his throat.

Sterling whispered in her ear, "Fairer than any."

Her eyes misted.

It had been a delightful day, and now she stood to one

side sipping her punch and watching her friends. Letty's whole family was there, as were Mary Beth and Ross, Glory and Kent, Iris and Lex, Veronica and Max, Parker and Georgie, along with all their children. It was a great community that was being formed. The best part was the Union Army had at last left Spring Water for good. That was another reason to celebrate.

"You look pensive, my love. Is something bothering you?" Sterling asked after he kissed her cheek.

"No, I was thinking about our many blessings. And the blessings I know are to come."

"Amen to that." He drew her into his arms and kissed her. He smiled and sang

COME OVER THE HILLS, *my bonnie Irish lass*
    Come over the hills to your darling
    You choose the road, love, and I'll make the vow
    And I'll be your true love forever.

RED IS *the rose that in yonder garden grows*
    Fair is the lily of the valley
    Clear is the water that flows from the Boyne
    But my love is fairer than any.

'TWAS DOWN *by Killarney's green woods that we strayed*
    When the moon and the stars they were shining
    The moon shone its rays on her locks of golden hair
    And she swore she'd be my love forever

. . .

RED IS the rose that in yonder garden grows
    Fair is the lily of the valley
    Clear is the water that flows from the Boyne
    But my love is fairer than any

AUTHOR NOTE

I hope you enjoyed all six books in this series. It has been an enlightening journey for me. Most people love the series but to some I'm not Christian enough. I'm Catholic with a big heart who gives so much more than I get but that's fine. I don't do it for praise or to win points with God. I made sure to make the book clean but it wasn't enough. I had my characters pray from their hearts still it wasn't good enough. I tried to tackle thinks such as forgiveness and judgement and of course everything a person does is between them and the Lord. People were so mean spirited I questioned myself and my relationship with God. Perhaps I wasn't a good Christian and I went in search of what exactly a Christian is. In the end my Priest showed me that it's the ones passing mean, cruel judgements on a book who should look inside themselves. Christians don't act that way. There is no hierarchy in Christianity despite what some seem to think. I do appreciate all of you who left positive reviews and sent me messages and email. I have come to the conclusion that I am enough. I am a child of God and that is enough.

My next series will be about the Oregon Trail. It will be a

sweet series and yes they will pray but I'm not sure I will call it Christian. God loves me and is always with me and right now that's all I need to know. Thank you all from the bottom of my heart for reading my books. It means the world to me.

Kathleen Ball

ABOUT THE AUTHOR

Sexy Cowboys and the Women Who Love Them...
Finalist in the 2012 and 2015 RONE Awards.
Top Pick, Five Star Series from the Romance Review.
Kathleen Ball writes contemporary and historical western
romance with great emotion and
memorable characters. Her books are award winners and
have appeared on best sellers lists including: Amazon's Best
Seller's List, All Romance Ebooks, Bookstrand, Desert
Breeze Publishing and Secret Cravings Publishing Best
Sellers list. She is the recipient of eight Editor's Choice
Awards, and The Readers' Choice Award for Ryelee's
Cowboy.
Winner of the Lear diamond award Best Historical Novel-
Cinders' Bride
There's something about a cowboy

facebook.com/kathleenballwesternromance

twitter.com/kballauthor

instagram.com/author_kathleenball

OTHER BOOKS BY KATHLEEN

Lasso Spring Series

Callie's Heart

Lone Star Joy

Stetson's Storm

Dawson Ranch Series

Texas Haven

Ryelee's Cowboy

Cowboy Season Series

Summer's Desire

Autumn's Hope

Winter's Embrace

Spring's Delight

Mail Order Brides of Texas

Cinder's Bride

Keegan's Bride

Shane's Bride

Tramp's Bride

Poor Boy's Christmas

Oregon Trail Dreamin'

We've Only Just Begun

A Lifetime to Share

A Love Worth Searching For

So Many Roads to Choose

The Settlers

Greg

Juan

Scarlett

Mail Order Brides of Spring Water

Tattered Hearts

Shattered Trust

Glory's Groom

Battered Soul

Faltered Beginnings

Fairer Than Any

The Greatest Gift

Love So Deep

Luke's Fate

Whispered Love

Love Before Midnight

I'm Forever Yours

Finn's Fortune

Glory's Groom

Made in the USA
Coppell, TX
10 May 2020

24931206R00095